Autumn Falling

A UFC ROMANTIC COMEDY

BLAIR MONROY

Autumn Falling

Copyright © 2024 Blair Monroy

All rights reserved.

Cover design by Aiden Kings

Books by Blair Monroy

GIRL FIGHT SERIES

Girl Fight

Spring Blues

Summer Storm

Autumn Falling

To gold diggers everywhere.

Contents

Playlist

EVA'S

LOVE STORY | TAYLOR SWIFT

KISS ME | SIXPENCE NONE THE RICHER

TÚ | SHAKIRA

ENCHANTED | TAYLOR SWIFT

ESPRESSO | SABRINA CARPENTER

SOMEWHERE ONLY WE KNOW | KEANE

WINTER'S BALLAD | CUCO

ERIC'S

STUCK LIKE GLUE | SUGARLAND

AMOR DE SIEMPRE | CUCO

IN YOUR EYES | PETER GABRIEL

LOVE WINS | CARRIE UNDERWOOD

YOU MAKE LOVING FUN | FLEETWOOD MAC

I DON'T WANT TO MISS A THING | AEROSMITH

LOVE | KENDRICK LAMAR

CHAPTER

ONE

KNEAD, KNEAD, KNEAD. REPEAT.

The air was 90% butter at this point—if I lit a match, the whole café would've gone up in a flambé of frustration. Dawn hadn't just broken; it had tripped and face-planted into the window, casting a pathetic gray glow over the countertops. My eyelids sagged like sandy balloons. I wasn't built for mornings like this. My body still thought it was 2 a.m., itching for a bad taco stand and a tummy ache of *regret*.

Felicia, meanwhile, was thriving. She pirouetted around the kitchen like Ina Garten on espresso, tarts and muffins emerging from the oven as if by magic—golden, flaky, and smugly perfect. I half-expected them to wink at me.

Then it hit me: this wasn't Guy's café anymore. It was *ours*. The realization hit like a rogue baguette to the face. I kneaded at the dough like it signed my paychecks, praying it'd morph into something that didn't resemble a fossilized pancake.

"You're nailing it," Felicia chirped, though her side-eye screamed "I've seen toddlers with better motor skills."

I wished I shared her delusion. Seven attempts. Seven disasters. Attempt 1) a crumbly mess that could've doubled as sand art. Attempt 2) a soggy blob that even the café's resident mouse (RIP, Keith) would've side-eyed. Attempt 3) over-kneaded into a rubbery brick. "Eva, gluten's a rule, not a suggestion," Felicia had sighed, as if I'd insulted her entire ancestry.

I'd nodded solemnly, like I hadn't spent weeks over-kneading my *entire life* into a sad, stretchy mess. My existence was basically a gluten-free pretzel at this point—all the effort, none of the structure.

"That's what you said when I burned the croissants," I muttered, blowing flour off my nose. I looked less "artisan baker" and more "Puritan ghost who'd died mid-bake-off." The white powder coated everything—my apron, my hair, *my will to live*.

And the worst part? I still couldn't wrap my head around how I'd gone from "Eva enjoys Saturday cortados by the window table" to "Eva, co-owner of a café she's one bad batch away from torching." Life had become a whirlwind, all right. And not the fun kind.

Felicia had executed the con of the century, and I'd been about as observant as a potted plant. For two years, she'd played me like a fiddle, cozying up to Guy—the café's former owner—like a Bond villain negotiating world domination. Month by month, she'd funneled cash into a secret "Buy the Café" fund, sacrificing what I can only assume was her entire shoe budget *and* her will to live. And Guy? That sly old fox had pocketed the cash, tossed her the keys, and bolted to a retirement village where his biggest daily challenge was now beating Mildred at bingo. Meanwhile, our lattes were still funding his shuffleboard habit.

We'd officially become "business owners" three weeks ago. Felicia was thriving, buzzing around like she'd been mainlining espresso since birth. Me? I was one misplaced muffin away from a full existential meltdown. I wanted to be useful—really!—but after two weeks of botching orders and accidentally switching out oat milk for non-fat, I'd been demoted to… *baking*.

Ah, baking. My true calling—if my calling involved dough that could double as hockey pucks and a soufflé that sighed like a disappointed parent. My medical (*pfft*) career? Useless here, unless someone needed a PowerPoint on why over-kneading causes carpal tunnel.

Next up: the coffee machine. A foolproof plan! Except the La Marzocco took one look at me and went full *Exorcist*, spewing grounds like it was auditioning for a horror film. Felicia, ever the cheerleader, suggested I "ease in" with the Mastrena instead. That relic shuddered like it was having a midlife crisis, and she yanked the plug before it could yeet itself into the afterlife. "It's never done that before!" she cried, sweat beading on her brow.

"It's not that I don't trust you with the machines," Felicia said later, in a tone that screamed "I'd trust a toddler with a chainsaw first." "It's just... maybe stick to... measuring things?"

So here I was, elbow-deep in flour, channeling my inner Ina Garten while secretly wondering if "home baking experience" was code for "once burned toast and cried." Felicia hovered nearby, her smile strained as she mentally tallied the cost of my sixth failed crust attempt. "You'll get the hang of it!" she said, with the forced optimism of someone watching their life savings evaporate in butter.

We both knew the truth: if I kept this up, we'd be recouping losses by selling my "artisanal" dough bricks as doorstops.

"What if I stick to *not* baking?" I blurted, wedging myself between the oven and the fridge like a human panic attack.

The kitchen had shrunk to the size of a shoebox, and I was pretty sure the walls were judging me. A tiny voice in my head hissed, "You're hemorrhaging butter money, Eva!" but I drowned it out.

Felicia sighed like a disappointed teacher, flour drifting off her apron like confetti at a very sad party. "Eva, sweetie, you're a *co-owner* now. You can't just... chill."

I slumped against the counter, my energy levels rivaling a sloth on melatonin. "It'd be easier to 'chill' if I hadn't been ambushed by this whole 'surprise, you're a business mogul' plot twist. I'm still waiting for the tutorial level!"

It wasn't just the secret café coup. It was the *financial carnage* she'd hidden until the last minute—maxed-out credit cards, drained savings, and a spreadsheet that looked like a horror movie budget. Suddenly, my life savings were less "retirement fund" and more "desperation fund."

"At least Lexi's got her sugar daddy bankrolling her existential crisis," I grumbled. "I've got... this." I gestured to my dried out dough.

Felicia, ever the optimist, insisted fear was "counterproductive." "Leaping blindly builds character!" she'd declared, as if we were starring in a motivational poster titled "BossBabe: A Cautionary Tale."

Truthfully, I'd fantasized about quitting my soul-sucking

medical job for years—usually during meetings about paperclip procurement or angry patient protocol. The café was my escape hatch, my fresh start, my… oh god, why is this pie crust *sweating*?

"It's not rocket science," Felicia said, poking my dough like an EOD bomb expert.

"No, it's worse," I snapped. "Rocket scientists don't have to worry about gluten tantrums!"

Felicia finally had enough and snatched the dough from my hands, transforming it into actual pie crusts with the precision of a pastry wizard. I stood there, coated in flour and inadequacy, feeling about as useful as a sentient breadcrumb. Her hands danced over the dough—graceful, practiced, infuriating—while mine still struggled with the concept of "knead, don't murder."

Somewhere beyond my existential crisis, the café door jingled. My heart rate spiked faster than Felicia's eyebrow.

"Eric's here," she muttered, in a tone full of frustration. He'd become a *frequent flier* at the café lately, popping in for "just a coffee" (it was never just a coffee). I lived for it. Felicia? She'd sooner adopt a feral cat.

I frantically swiped flour off my apron, which only made me look like I'd lost a fight with a ghost, and fluffed my hair into something resembling "I tried."

"We're *closed*," I announced, leaning against the counter with faux professionalism. "Health code violation. Rogue yeast epidemic. It's tragic, really."

He kept advancing, all smirks and biceps and *good lord, how do sweats look that illegal*? His grin was a lethal combo of boyish charm and "I know exactly what you're thinking."

"Perfect," he said, closing the gap between us like a man on a mission.

Before I could squeak "public decency laws!", he hoisted me up, and I instinctively clamped my legs around his waist. His lips met mine, soft and warm and *oh hello, serotonin*. Being petite had its perks—like spontaneous airborne kisses.

I tangled my fingers in his hair, which was unfairly silky for someone who spent 90% of his time punching bags, and stole another kiss. When he finally set me down, his hands lingered on my hips like they'd found their forever home. Letting myself *like* him—let alone *slobber* him—had taken approximately 47 years of therapy (and one mortifying viral video involving Tegan, a wayward "disgusting pig" comment, and a very confused Eric). But here we were.

Progress.

Hot, sweaty, possibly *indecent* progress.

He pulled me into a hug that could've doubled as a bear trap, his voice a low rumble in my ear about missing me, thinking about me mid-kickboxing, and *wouldn't a weekend getaway be nice?* His hands slid under my apron, tracing my spine like he was memorizing it for an exam.

"For the love of god, get a room!" Felicia barked, storming in with the energy of a disapproving nun. "Some of us are trying to run a business here, not star in a softcore baking show."

"That's the plan," Eric fired back, grinning as he laced his fingers through mine. His thumb brushed my palm, sparking a shiver that could've powered the café's espresso machine.

He was joking.

Mostly.

Eric and I had officially entered the "Will They/Won't They" phase of our relationship—a rom-com trope so cliché, even Netflix would've rolled its eyes. Sure, we'd established that we were, biologically speaking, *extremely* compatible. But actual *full-body togetherness*? That required navigating my anxiety and a "slow burn" pace that would've made Jane Austen yell, "Get on with it!"

Painfully slow, if you will.

Honestly, I wasn't sure if I was savoring the tension or

just emotionally stalling. (Translation: Why not both?) Watching him unravel was delightful—the way his jaw twitched when I "accidentally" grazed his neck, the way his hands flexed like he was mentally measuring the nearest horizontal surface. And the touching? Soft, teasing strokes that left me vibrating like a poorly balanced washing machine.

"Eva?"

Felicia's voice sliced through my X-rated daydream like a nun with a ruler.

"Hmm?" I croaked, fanning myself with a menu. "Is it just me, or is it *sweltering* in here?"

"I said," Felicia deadpanned, "Lexi and Tegan called an emergency PR meeting. Tomorrow. They want us to 'consult' on their new product launch."

I blinked. "Why? We're in the PR list, not their PR *team*." (Last week, their *very important* meeting had been a series of back and forth between Tegan and Lexi that had amounted to, let's see—two plus two equals—nothing!) Plus, Eric's "weekend getaway" idea was sounding far more appealing than playing focus group to Lexi's chaos.

Felicia smirked. "Obviusly, this is about Tegan's divorce. The Subreddit's blowing up—Scott's in Phuket with some 'yoga instructor' who's definitely a CIA spy," she said, tossing Eric a cookie like she was feeding a zoo animal. He'd mastered the art of existing near our gossip—hovering silently, snacking stoically, pretending not to know Charles once tried to trademark "Broody McAbs" as a cologne.

"But Tegan's divorcing Scott!" I protested. "Why does she care if he's flirting with a CIA spy?"

"Because pride," Felicia said, as if that explained everything. "And Charles is now undercover as Scott's 'ride or die' to trick him into getting arrested for tax fraud. All to win Lexi back."

I jerked upright. "What the hell are you on about? I didn't hear *any* of this."

Felicia rolled her eyes. "Obviously not. You've been too busy mentally undressing Eric in every conceivable location —the stockroom, the walk-in freezer, the *out of order* bathroom—"

"I have not!" I squeaked, my face flaming hotter than a Cheeto.

I risked a glance at Eric behind the counter, who was now leaning against the espresso machine, casually demolishing a cookie with a smirk that screamed "Liar, liar, apron on fire."

"Just bang him already!" Felicia bellowed, like a Shakespearean herald announcing a royal decree. "You've been about as useful as a decaf espresso since he started giving you those *looks*. Eric, since you're eavesdropping like a TMZ reporter—do the world a favor and put us all out of our misery. Most of all, Eva. Please."

Eric prowled over, his gaze locked on mine like a heat-seeking missile. "Anytime," he purred, voice smoother than a triple-shot latte. Then he winked—*the audacity*—and I knew he couldn't wait until I caved or spontaneously combusted. Whichever came first.

I bit back a grin, my cheeks now matching the café's emergency exit sign. "Can we *not* act like we're filming *Naked Attraction*? Some of us have jobs to get to!"

"Fine," Felicia huffed, slamming a palm onto the counter. "Let's talk budgets. Thrilling, I know."

Eric dipped down, brushing a kiss against my lips so soft I nearly forgot my own name. "Too good to be true," he murmured, pulling back just enough to make my knees wobble. "Call you later."

"Later," I breathed, swaying slightly as he left.

Felicia snapped her fingers in front of my face. "Focus! We're hemorrhaging money faster than Lexi burns through shoes. Guy's tarts funded his retirement villa, and our 'viral fame' lasted about as long as a Snapchat streak."

I groaned. "I told you hashtags aren't a business plan."

"What if we make another viral video?" Felicia said, waving a whisk like a magic wand. "You know… shirtless firemen? Puppies in aprons? Something?"

Suddenly, my old lifeguard-and-bottle-service hustler brain sparked. "What if we host a UFC meet-and-greet? Eric and his buddies, signing autographs… in tank tops?"

Felicia froze, her eyes widening like she'd just spotted a unicorn. "Genius. But only if you promise to finally—"

"No."

"Eva, if he agrees to this, you owe it to humanity to climb that man like a *tree*."

I choked on my laugh. "Stop!"

"It's basic karma!" she insisted, grinning like the Cheshire Cat. "The universe demands it."

Maybe it does, I thought, biting my lip. *And maybe the universe is onto something.*

CHAPTER

TWO

THE SECOND I HEARD "I wish grandpas never died" twanging through the office speakers, I knew—Claire had "mysteriously" called out again. That meant one of the doctors' wives was manning the front desk, and because no one else here subjected patients to Riley Green Greatest Hits playlist, I knew it was Reina. Honestly, the woman treated Morgan Wallen like a religion. If I heard "Last Night" one more time, I'd start drafting a restraining order against the Bluetooth speaker.

What *did* shock me was Reina's punctuality. Her husband, Dr. "I Don't Do Mornings Before My Third Espresso," usually scheduled his first patient at 9:15 a.m.— just late enough to justify Reina's "traffic was a nightmare" fib. But there she was, at 8:58 a.m., tapping her manicured nails to "Dirt Road Anthem" like she'd been raised in a

Nashville honky-tonk.

Claire's return to work post-baby had been a saga worthy of a Lifetime movie. First, she'd tried daycare, but lasted exactly 1.5 days before spiraling into a "what if they feed my child non-organic pears?!" panic. Then she'd strong-armed her mom into early retirement with a guilt trip so masterful, Lexi would've saluted. "All I did was mention how strangers kissed the baby," Claire had whispered to me, grinning like a Bond villain. "And *poof*—suddenly she's buying a crib."

But deep down, Claire wanted to be a stay-at-home mom. Instead, she'd become the Picasso of phantom sick days. First, a "24-hour COVID" (symptoms: needing a nap). Then a "migraine" that coincided with her baby's third monthiversary. The woman was gaming the system like it was Grand Theft Auto: Paid Leave Edition.

I was restocking tongue depressors when Lexi popped her head in, humming "Fancy Like" with the confidence of someone who'd never actually eaten at Applebee's.

"Heard about the Formula 1 drama?" she asked, tossing a glove dispenser like it was a bouquet.

"Formula 1… the salad dressing?" I said, squinting.

Lexi cackled so hard she nearly toppled a skeleton model. "The car race, you doughnut! Max Verstappen's dating a pop star now. It's chaos. Charles is fuming."

"Why? Did he want to date the pop star?"

"No! Charles thinks Verstappen'll be distracted," she deadpanned. "Men are weird."

I shrugged. "And this affects my life... how? Are they racing through the Target parking lot?"

"Ugh, Eva," Lexi groaned, like I'd just confessed to ironing my socks. "It's on the *Strip*! Charles splurged on VIP tickets months ago. No more jetting off to Monaco—this time, the ultra-rich are coming to *us*. Cha-ching!"

"How... efficient," I said, imagining Monaco as a glittery utopia of yachts and men named Pierre. "Since when do you care about cars? You still think torque is a type of meat."

She shot me a look sharper than her contour. "It's not about the cars, you walnut. It's about the men driving them—or, better yet, the men *funding* them. TFMAMs (Trust Fund Middle-Aged Men™) with Rolexes and trust funds thicker than Charles' skull."

"Ah, right. Your 'Trust Fund Middle-Aged Men' initiative," I said, nodding sagely. "Must be exhausting vetting new candidates for 'old' and 'loaded.' Do they get a loyalty card?"

"Backups, darling. Always have backups," she purred,

nudging me like we were co-conspirators in a heist. "And let's face it—Brody's more 'backup dancer' than 'backup plan.'"

She cackled at her own joke, but let's be real: if Brody were a snack, he'd be a dangerously over-salted cracker—thrilling in small doses, but guaranteed to leave you parched and regretful. Sure, he had the abs of a Greek statue and the charm of a Labrador, but his temper? Let's just say he could flip from "sweetheart" to "scream-queen" faster than Lexi could say "Champagne problems."

"Does Brody know he's bench warming for Charles 2.0?" I asked. "Last time he caught a whiff of your 'commitment issues,' he nearly redecorated the café with a fist."

I'd seen that glint in Brody's eye when he drank—which was often, like he was auditioning for *Celebrity Rehab: Vegas Edition*. Lexi waved it off with a breezy "He's reformed!" but I wasn't buying it. The man had the emotional stability of the economy.

"Relax," Lexi said, rolling her eyes. "He's fine. Besides, Charles is practically begging to fund my next 'incident.'"

I bit my tongue. Brody wasn't *fine*. He was a lit firework, and Lexi was tossing around matches like confetti. But try telling her that.

"Does *he* know that?"

"Yes, Eva. Brody knows," Lexi declared, waving a hand like she was swatting a pesky fly. "He's strictly for *recreational use* now. We've had lengthy talks—think TED Talks, but with more bedsheets and fewer clothes. He's my stress ball. With biceps." She grabbed her clipboard, signaling the conversation was as dead as last year's eyelash extensions. "But Charles? Ugh. He's like a strong WiFi signal—I keep reconnecting!"

"I may not be a crystal ball, but I think it's his money," I quipped, rolling my stool closer.

"He gives me money even when we're not together, silly."

"Shocking." But it wasn't, really.

She set her bundle of supplies down, ready to drop some gossip bombs. "Babe, the man's been unstoppable. He's been funding my lifestyle like it's his civic duty, that's nothing new. It's the late-night sushi deliveries for me. A personal shopper named Cara who cries if I don't buy the beige? Done. And the *pièce de résistance*—" She paused, savoring the drama. "A Kelly bag so real, it's practically came with an invite to the Met Gala."

I glanced at the bag hanging off her chair—the one the receptionists called "Faux-liwood's finest" behind her back. Little did they know, Charles had likely mortgaged his soul to afford it. Lexi could sniff out a counterfeit from a mile away, like a truffle pig for designer leather.

"But wait—" She leaned in, voice dropping to a whisper usually reserved for unsavory gossip. "I've upped the ante. If he wants me back, I want him to drag Scott back from Thailand. Alive. Or mildly sunburned. Either works."

"*What?*" I choked, nearly upending my coffee. "Scott's been off-grid since *Forbes* called him the 'crypto Yeti!'"

"Exactly!" Lexi's grin was pure mischief. "Charles is going to sweet-talk him into surrendering—using Scott's *own* offshore cash. It's *Ocean's Eleven* meets *Golden Bachelor*! And if Charles pulls it off? I might actually forgive him. Maybe.

"This is unhinged," I muttered, equal parts horrified and weirdly impressed. "What if Scott's, I don't know, happy sipping mojitos in Phuket?"

"Happy?" Lexi scoffed. "He's hiding in a beach shack, Eva. The man's funds are frozen. This is a mercy mission."

"How's Charles going to pull that off?"

Lexi straightened up, preening like she'd just won a fight. "Babe, I'm not lifting a manicured finger—Charles is doing all the heavy lifting. His grand gesture or *buh-bye*. Simple."

"Wow," I said, equal parts horrified and weirdly impressed. "But how's Charles even going to find Scott? Last

I heard, he moves around like—well, a man in hiding. And besides, isn't he broker than Bernie Madoff."

"Don't be naive," Lexi scoffed, flicking her hair like a Regency heroine dismissing a suitor. "Scott didn't lose *his* money—just everyone else's. That's why he's technically a fugitive and not just an idiot in hiding. If Charles drags him back, I'll marry him in a drive-thru chapel if I have to. And the cash? Mine. Finder's fee, baby."

"So you're… romantic blackmailers?"

"Partners in profit," she corrected, grinning. "Once Tegan's off the hook, she's funneling that divorce cash into our skincare line. Smart, right?"

I'd officially clocked out of productivity, leaning against the counter like this was a post-work wine chat. "But why wait? Can't you two just Venmo each other?"

Lexi groaned, as if I'd suggested pairing socks with sandals. "Do you have any clue how much an all *pink* office costs? Or liability insurance? We're broke, Eva. Charles would bankroll me, but then he'd want his logo on our serum bottles. 'Clinically tested by septuagenarian wrinkly balls'— hard pass."

She paused, a laugh bubble escaping. "Besides, Tegan's sex tape *flopped*. Turns out, nobody pays for nudes when they can screenshot. Rookie mistake."

"Sex tapes aren't really my area," I mumbled. "But I know how expensive businesses can be—firsthand."

She scoffed. "That sad little café? Please. Just bat those doe eyes at Eric and let him bankroll it. If he's that smitten, he'll Venmo you his life savings before you finish a cortado. You know my motto—" She paused, waiting for me to parrot the mantra she'd drilled into me since I met her.

"A man's wallet is his love language," I recited dryly.

"Exactly," she purred. "If he lets you drown in debt while he's off punching bags two doors down? Drop him. Real love is Venmo notifications and surprise Amex gifts."

I slumped, wondering if I had it in me. Life *would* be easier if I could channel my inner Lexi—a woman who'd ask a stranger for their kidney *and* a five-star Yelp review. But no, I'd been raised by parents who thought "self-sufficiency" was a superhero trait. *Yawn*.

"Plus, you're sitting on a goldmine," she added, gesturing to my body like it was a dormant oil rig. "You haven't even kissed him properly yet. The power! The leverage!"

"I'm not withholding affection for benefits," I hissed, cheeks blazing.

"Why not?" She leaned in, eyes glittering. "Men swap

loyalty points for far less. We're out here playing house while they're running *Wolf of Wall Street* marathons with a different Barbie every week. Time to flip the script, babe."

"Or… hear me out—I want love, not money?"

Lexi snorted, waving a hand adorned with a ring Charles probably bought *during* their last breakup. "You talk like someone who's never had more than a $10 bill. Money's not evil, Eva—it's just like high-quality oxygen. And you're over here gasping like a nun on a rollercoaster."

"I'm fine with my regular oxygen, thanks," I muttered, though part of me wondered if she had a point. My savings account resembled a sad origami swan, while Eric's probably had its own TikTok account.

"Sure you are," she said, smirking. "But when your espresso machine explodes *again*, and Eric's just there, looking like a *GQ* ad feeling sorry for you? Don't come crying to me. He either opens his wallet or he goes, that's my motto."

I pictured it—Eric, all smoldering sincerity, offering to fix the café's sputtering espresso machine. *Tempting.* But then I remembered my mother's voice: "Independence is everything for a woman, Eva!"

"I'll stick to my budget handbag," I said, marching out

before she could counter.

"Don't give it away for free, babe!" she trilled after me.

Lexi wasn't entirely wrong. Even Felicia had hinted at my "untapped potential," though her version involved me weaponizing my celibacy à la *Crazy Ex-Girlfriend*—shared location, phone passcode and all. "He's obsessed because you're a *challenge*," she'd said, as if dating were a UFC match and I was out here scoring points by not texting back immediately. "He'd do anything you say, trust me."

Lexi's take? "Make him fund the café. Men love projects —it's why they date us."

Their advice clashed like fire and ice, but both left me wondering: Was I sitting on a goldmine of unclaimed power or just a landfill of overthink?

For me, it wasn't about transactional tit-for-tat—"You get a kiss, I get a new espresso machine!"—but about not morphing into someone who'd trade self-respect for a Birkin. Still, the idea buzzed in my brain like a trapped wasp.

What if I could nudge Eric into hosting a UFC meet-and-greet at the café? Felicia swore he'd do it for a kiss. Lexi swore he'd do it for *less*.

"It's not manipulation," Felicia argued. "It's a… strategic upper hand."

"It's *survival*," Lexi corrected. "And if he's into it? Free bills, baby."

But then I imagined Eric's face—all earnest smiles and "I'd do anything for you" eyes—and guilt curdled my stomach.

Lexi's version of empowerment involved penthouse views and men who doubled as ATMs. Mine? Not so much. But as I scraped burnt croissant scraps off a tray at my second shift, I couldn't help but wonder: What if "self-respect" and "free marketing" weren't mutually exclusive?

CHAPTER

THREE

SUMMER VANISHED FASTER THAN a margarita at a pool party, leaving behind nothing but a sunburned memory and a few rogue flip-flops. The sky still blazed blue, but the heat had finally stopped hulking over us like a gym bro on steroids. 80º f now felt practically arctic—locals were out here layering on cardigans and sipping pumpkin spice lattes like it was the Harvest Moon in Maine.

Autumn was trying, bless its heart. No falling leaves, just a few half-hearted gusts of wind that mostly blew sand into everyone's iced coffees. But Vegas had decided this was "outdoor weather," and suddenly, the entire city had descended upon Desert Bloom like seagulls on a taco truck.

Was it Lexi's Instagram post—"New Owners, Same Chaos"—that went viral? Or Felicia's Subreddit sleuths, who'd somehow doxxed our espresso machine? Who knew.

All I knew was that the café had become the valley's *other* hottest ticket. Not because of our life-changing lemon tarts (though, *hello*, they're sublime), but because we'd accidentally become a reality TV episode. Lexi held court at the corner table, posing like she was auditioning for *Real Housewives: Business Babe Edition*. Eric "accidentally" shirtless polished the espresso machine (don't ask). And Tegan? She'd turned her perch by the window into a live-stream throne, narrating her "humble new chapter" with the gravitas of a reformed gold digger.

Tegan and I weren't exactly friends, either, but water under the bridge! Or, in her case, champagne under the yacht? She'd bounced back from her "divorce era" with the resilience of a cockroach in a nuclear winter, and my friends? They'd welcomed her with open arms and open tabs. Couldn't blame them. Drama was Lexi's love language, and Tegan was *fluent*.

The café was heaving. Our till was *cha-chinging* like a slot machine on a winning streak, and I should've been thrilled. Instead, I was mentally calculating how many avocado toasts it would take to fix the AC before next summer (answer: 12,000). Sure, the crowds were here for the "show"—but money was money. Even if my bank account still had more holes than Brody's gym socks.

Lexi had a front-row seat to my daily meltdowns and

declared it "high time" for Eric to swoop in like a knight in shining Amex. "If you're gonna have a man, make him pay," she'd say, sipping her nonfat latte like it was liquid wisdom. "Otherwise, you're just a self-sufficient sucker."

But asking Eric for cash felt like ordering a salad at a steakhouse—technically possible, but deeply unnatural. Lexi swore he'd be thrilled ("Men live for this! It's their love language!"), but my gut screamed, "Abort mission!" So I white-knuckled through another month, my savings evaporating faster than Lexi's patience for non-VIP events.

Keeping the café alive was like running a marathon in heels—glamorous in theory, disastrous in practice. Mornings: diagnosing hypochondriacs. Evenings: diagnosing why the espresso machine wept like a soap opera widow. By midnight, I was a sentient to-do list, dreaming of a life where "double shift" meant *two naps*.

Felicia, meanwhile, floated through her days like Martha Steward on Prozac. To her, the café was a symphony of muffins and gossip. To me? A never-ending game of *Whack-a-Mole* with bills. She'd hum while piping rosettes onto cupcakes; I'd whimper while Googling "Can you sell a kidney on eBay?"

"You're a natural!" Felicia chirped, as I botched my tenth croissant.

"At failure? Absolutely," I muttered, wondering if "artisanal charcoal loaf" could trend on TikTok.

I hadn't chosen this life—it chose me, like a stray cat that won't stop vomiting on your rug. Felicia's dream was my obligation, a Pinterest board come to life that I was forced to glue-gun. I loved her tarts, but baking them? Hard pass. I adored the café's vibe, but serving? Exhausting.

Yet here I was—part-time barista, full-time martyr—praying for a miracle (or a lottery win) while Lexi side-eyed my "principles" like they were last season's handbags.

"One ask, Eva!" she'd hiss. "Just flutter those lashes and say 'Baby, the AC's broke—also, my soul?'"

Maybe next month. Or maybe I'd just live in the walk-in freezer.

Such was my *glamorous* new life—trapped in a business I never asked for, hemorrhaging cash like a tapas bar with a Groupon. Quitting? Impossible. I'd sunk my savings into this place, and Felicia? She'd just asked for more to cover Shane's salary—a man who treated punctuality like a suggestion, not a virtue. "He's our MVP!" she'd chirped, as if "Most Valuable Procrastinator" was a real award.

"Shift your mindset!" Felicia urged.

Cali, sister and resident pregnant bump, nodded.

"Mindset's 50% of success!" she trilled. Right. The other 50%? Desperation, caffeine, and a prayer circle for the espresso machine.

Mine currently oscillated between "raging inferno" and "numb void." I'd mastered the art of smiling through gritted teeth while fantasizing about tossing Felicia's sourdough starter into the sun.

The only silver lining? Eric. If I could've spent my days here without the medical office grind, maybe I'd bump into him more—casual run-ins, flirty banter, his biceps accidentally ripping another apron. But no, I was stuck playing real-life Tetris with my schedule, while my brain helpfully supplied *very* NSFW daydreams about his hands, his smile, his—

"Earth to Eva!" Lexi's voice sliced through my X-rated mental montage. "You're doing the thing again—the face. The one where you mentally undress Eric. Which, *same*, but maybe wait till your shift ends?"

Her laugh was a mix of champagne bubbles and subtle shaming. Lexi's arrival always drew a crowd—part influencer, part tornado—and today was no exception. The café buzzed, customers pretending not to eavesdrop as they Instagrammed their lattes.

"I'm memorizing recipes," I lied, waving Felicia's coffee

guide like a prop. "Turns out 'espresso' doesn't mean 'cry into the beans.' Who knew?"

Lexi rolled her eyes. "Please. Eric just walked in looking like a sweaty Greek statue come to life, and you're over here blushing like a Victorian heroine. Just *do* him already. If you won't let him fund your nervous breakdown, at least let him distract you."

The room tilted. Was she right? Maybe. But the idea of using Eric—or letting him use me—felt as icky as day-old croissant crumbs.

"Not everything's a transaction, Lex," I muttered, rearranging muffins like they'd judge me.

"Says the woman who still pays for her own Netflix," she shot back, sauntering off to "accidentally" photobomb Tegan's live stream.

"For the love of god, make it stop," Felicia hissed, balancing a tray of muffins like a waitress in a sitcom. "Your unresolved sexual tension is giving me hives. And not the cute, rom-com kind—the *urgent care* kind."

"Stop," I whispered, cheeks flaming like a malfunctioning toaster.

Felicia arched a brow. "Tegan's here. So maybe shelve the Eric thirst traps? She's not exactly your biggest fan."

"Wait—" My pulse spiked, anger bubbling up like over proofed dough. "Is she still into him?" I glared at Tegan, who was hosting a live.

"God, no," Lexi said, not looking up. "She's into self-destruction and cashmere now."

"Then why tip-toe? And let's not forget she *literally* stole my boyfriend *and* got me fired!" My voice climbed an octave, sharp enough to slice through Felicia's sourdough.

Felicia pressed a flour-dusted finger to her lips. "Eva. Honey. Tegan's life is a Netflix cautionary tale. Her husband's gone ghost, her credit score's in the ICU. Cut her some slack."

Lexi snorted. "Slack? Tegan wouldn't cut *you* slack if you were dangling off the Eiffel Tower."

"Plus," Felicia added, lowering her voice to a whisper usually reserved for discussing expired milk, "the Subreddit's saying *you* stole Eric. That you're, like, a home-wrecking cupcake or something."

"Stole him?!" I barked, loud enough to startle a customer into spilling their matcha. "She stole my whole life. She's literally a crime!"

Tegan, piped in, her live ending. "Still hung up on ancient history, Eva?" she purred, examining her nails like they held stock options. "It's *pathetic*, really."

I shot Felicia a "told you so" glare hot enough to roast coffee beans. "Felicia thinks my relationship bothers you. But you're fine, right? You've moved on to greener pastures, right?"

Lexi caught my eye, her expression screaming "Abort mission," but Felicia—ever the chaos gremlin—tossed a verbal grenade. "But *is* he your man? You haven't even *done the deed*. Is he… waiting for a receipt?"

I white-knuckled the counter, fantasizing about catapulting a muffin at her head. "That's not the point," I hissed, my voice slicing through the café's cozy ambiance like a sword through bread.

Tegan, meanwhile, lounged against the counter like a bored sphinx, buffing her nails on her *allegedly* vintage Chanel blazer. "Not this again," she sighed. "Sleep with him, don't sleep with him—I couldn't care less. Just have Eric slide me a UFC guy's number. Preferably one who knows what a prenup is."

"I'm not your personal Tinder!" I snapped, my patience evaporating faster than foam on a cappuccino.

"Non-fat latte and a lemon tart, Felicia," Lexi interjected, materializing between us like a popup. "Then join us. We've got business to discuss."

"Finally, something productive," Tegan said, commandeering my favorite window seat. Her phone glowed ominously, likely tracking her ex's crypto transactions or Googling "how to sue a Thai beach resort."

I gritted my teeth so hard I nearly cracked a molar. "Fine. But tell Tegan to back off before I 'accidentally' decaf her."

Lexi shot me a look. "She can hear you, Eva. Let's focus on the skincare line. You know, the thing that'll pay our bills?"

Tegan glanced up, smirking like she'd just won *Squid Games: Divorce Edition*. "Nonfat latte, raspberry tart, and hurry up. We're discussing margins, not your meltdown."

I exhaled loudly enough to rattle the cookie jar. Sweet merciful matcha, give me strength.

CHAPTER

FOUR

SOMEONE HAD WEDGED THE café door shut, trapping the lingering heat of the afternoon's bakes like a vengeful ghost haunting the register area. It felt like mid-June in a power outage, which—paired with Tegan's infuriating latte order—turned my mood from "mildly frazzled" to "actively plotting arson." Taylor Swift crooned about another ex-boyfriend in the background, while Shane—our barista with the patience of a hangry seagull—argued with a customer over caramel pumps.

"Seven pumps," the woman insisted, stabbing her cup. "This is five. I can *taste* the deficit."

"Haven't you heard," Shane retorted. "Caramel's a ration."

I breezed past, hot enough to spontaneously combust, and barked at him to fix it. Customer service was apparently my new calling, right up there with "unpaid therapist" and "emotional janitor."

Shane muttered something under his breath, but drizzled in two extra pumps anyway, earning a smug smirk from the customer. I wanted to smack her right into Sunday.

The café pulsed with busy bodies, each person clutching a drink and talking away like an extra in *Friends*. How were we *still* hemorrhaging money? We should've been rolling in cash like Mr. Krabs. Had the attitude down pat, didn't I.

"I'm fuming right now," I announced to Felicia, who stood in the back piping frosting onto cupcakes like this was her personal zen garden.

(Translation: It was.)

"Why?" she asked, genuinely baffled, as if the café weren't one spilled oat milk away from an OSHA investigation.

"Look at this place! It's a disaster! And your 'casual' jab about Eric in front of Tegan? She's been ordering raspberry tarts and lattes like she's the CEO of Passive-Aggressivia!"

Felicia let out a sigh so heavy it could've anchored a cruise ship, her eyes darting around the café like a meerkat on espresso. The place was packed—a rare miracle in the desert of midweek lulls—and she was in full "profit-orperish" mode. "Eva, can this wait? I'm literally drowning in capitalism right now, and you're… what's the opposite of a lifeguard? A lead brick?"

I planted my feet, mad and stubborn. "And how *exactly* am I supposed to help when I don't know the first thing about running a café? I know how to *order* coffee, not make it. I know how to enjoy it, not *own* the damn place. I'm like a penguin in a sandbox here!"

She brushed past me, eye roll barely contained, as she restocked the muffin display for the third time. The raspberry-lemon tarts were vanishing faster than my self-esteem, too. "Eva, I brought you into this to give you a lifeline, babe. You hate your job, you're always moaning about it. Now you're part owner, and what? You hate this too?" She threw her hands up, nearly decapitating a croissant. "I don't know what to tell you. But we're busy, so either grab a mop or *skedaddle*."

Shane, nodded solemnly before gently herding me aside like a lost sheep and delivering lattes to Lexi and Tegan, who were camped at *my* usual table.

I stood there, simmering like a teapot left on high. Okay, fine, I'd overreacted. But admitting that felt like swallowing a cactus. Humiliated, I slunk back to my table—now colonized by Lexi and Tegan, who were gushing over their skincare line like it was the Second Coming of Moisturizer. Normally, I'd fake interest. Today? I wanted to hurl a scone at their "toxin-free glow serum" pitch.

Everything felt upside-down. My life had become a Pinterest board designed by a drunk toddler, and I was *not* handling it with grace.

I was pissed. And not just at Tegan.

Maybe I was overwhelmed. Maybe I was *sexually frustrated*.

I shoved that thought into the mental vault labeled "Nope."

Brody had materialized at the counter, which meant Eric was seconds away. Normally, the sight of him would've sparked joy, but today? My brain was a browser with 110 tabs open. My *life* was a browser with 110 tabs open. And I'd forgotten the password to close any of them.

But one thing was clear: my happiness mattered more than Tegan's "comfort."

Silently, I dared her to poke me again.

That woman wouldn't know what hit her.

"I love licorice," Lexi declared, slapping a sample vial of serum onto the table. "If the lab can replicate this exact formula but make it, like, *juicier*, I'll sign my soul away.

Hydrate me, babe."

Tegan nodded, scribbling notes on her iPad with a stylus so aggressively I half-expected sparks. She was in full CEO mode, oblivious to my internal meltdown—or maybe just ignoring it.

Meanwhile, me?

It's me, hi, I'm the problem, it's me. (Thanks, Taylor Swift, for the theme song to my existential crisis.)

And then it hit me like a rogue piñata.

Everyone around me had their lives sorted: Felicia with her café empire, Lexi with her Dewy & Damaged™ skincare cult, even Tegan had somehow rebranded from "hot mess" to "hot CEO." And me? I was adrift in a sea of *what even am I doing?*

To add insult to injury, Eric had popped in earlier for a "quick hello" that lasted roughly 12 seconds. "Sorry, babe, gotta dash. Training's *intense*—just signed for another fight. You proud?" *Of course* I said yes. Then I watched him vanish with Brody, jabbering about "uppercuts" and "footwork" like they were solving world hunger.

Lexi, meanwhile, was shooting me death glares. Probably because after an *hour* of debating whether licorice serum should "tingle or *burn*," I'd finally snapped.

"What am I even doing here? I'm not on the PR team, and I don't know diddly squat about skincare unless 'don't rub lemon juice on your face' counts as expertise."

Lexi sighed like I'd just insulted her firstborn. "You're not on the PR team, Eva. We're in *development*."

I rolled my eyes into my brain. "Well, this feels like a development in how to waste my afternoon." I crossed my arms, channeling the energy of a sober grump.

Tegan cleared her throat, tiptoeing into the conversation like she was defusing a bomb. "Maybe Eva needs a break? She's been juggling *two* jobs, after all…"

I snorted. "What I *need* is to not be trapped in this meeting about a serum that'll probably give people rashes. Again."

I was fuming. Fuming that they'd dragged me into this glorified pyramid scheme funded by Tegan's sex tape residuals—which, let's be real, had the shelf life of gas station sushi roll. Kim K turned scandal into Skims; Tegan turned hers into a GoFundMe for bad decisions.

"And since your little tape tanked," I added, sharp as a stiletto, "maybe we should pivot to something realistic. Like, I don't know, *lip balm*? Or is that too ambitious?"

Lexi gasped. "Eva! It's niche!"

"Niche?" I shot back. "The only thing 'niche' here is your target audience: men who have to pay for it."

Silence.

Then Tegan's stylus snapped.

Tegan gasped so hard she nearly inhaled her latte, while Lexi's glare could've frozen hell.

"Okay," Lexi announced, slamming her untouched notebook shut with the finality of a reality TV elimination. "This meeting is *over* over."

Felicia, who'd been lurking like a nosy neighbor, sidled over. "Already? I didn't even get to participate!"

"Oh, we're done," Lexi replied, icier than a Yeti's toenails. Felicia shot me a "you've really done it now" look before retreating to the register—*traitor*.

Under the table, Lexi kicked my foot. "Can we talk?"

I met her stare, arms crossed like a petulant toddler. "Look, I know I'm being a brat, and I'm sorry, but I'm so stretched I could be Spandex. This meeting sucked my soul out through a straw."

Lexi dragged me to the back of the café—a place I was starting to associate with interventions and expired milk. "Maybe," she said, channeling Oprah, "you need a break."

"Maybe," I grumbled. "But everywhere I go, I'm just wallpaper. I can't bake, I'm skincare-clueless, and Eric and I are stuck in romantic purgatory. I can't even gold-dig properly because my *conscience* won't shut up. I'm basically third-wheeling my own life!"

Lexi nodded sagely, like she'd cracked the Da Vinci Code. "I know *exactly* what you're going to do."

I squinted. "What? Cry?"

"You're going to *work* Eric," she declared, slapping my back like a motivational coach.

I blinked. "Another job? I already hate my *two*!"

Lexi rolled her eyes. "No, dummy. *Gold-dig*. It's decided."

I choked. "Excuse me?"

"If you feel lost, take control," she said, as if this were profound and not deranged. "Money's the ultimate therapy. And Eric's rolling in it. So, dig. The universe is *screaming* at you to do it."

I gaped at her. "You want me to gold-dig Eric?"

"Exactly," Lexi purred, smirking like Cruella De Vil petting a Dalmatian. "When you're a gold digger, all your problems just... *poof*." She mimicked an explosion with her hands. "Gone. And honey, you need a *poof* the size of Mount

Vesuvius."

Something was deeply wrong with me, because her insanity was starting to sound logical. Like, alarmingly logical. My sanity was evacuating my brain like rats from a sinking ship.

"Tell me," Lexi pressed, eyes glinting like she'd just found a loophole in the Ten Commandments, "wouldn't your mood improve if Eric was funding your life? Imagine it— sipping margaritas in Bali while he Venmo's your landlord. *Bliss.*"

I arched a brow. "Maybe not my rent... but Shane's salary? The guy can't even spell 'cortado' without crying, but we need him."

Lexi's smirk morphed into a full-blown grin. "Now you're speaking my language."

I exhaled, half-tempted, half-horrified. "And how, exactly, do I pull this off without ending up on a true crime podcast?"

She leaned in, and right before my eyes, she transformed —shedding her civilian disguise. The Lexi I knew vanished, replaced by The Huntress™, a creature of pure chaos and sensuality. I'd seen her do this before, but never this close. It was like watching a magician reveal their trick... if the trick was stacking bills.

"You're going to do exactly what I tell you," she said, her voice a mix of silky and menacing, like a panther in Prada.

I gulped. *God help me.*

CHAPTER

FIVE

MY BEDROOM LOOKED LIKE an H&M had thrown up in it. Clothes were strewn everywhere—dresses slumped over chairs, jeans defying gravity on lampshades, a lone sock waving from the ceiling fan like a surrender flag. Nothing-looks-good syndrome had struck with the vengeance of a scorned ex, and I was losing the battle. Canceling was *not* an option (Translation: Lexi would murder me *dead* dead), and the weather had the audacity to be neutral. Not hot, not cold —just *blah*. Mother Nature was basically gaslighting my wardrobe.

Gold digger step one: look effortlessly hot.

Gold digger step two-ten: *panic*.

"What about this dress?" Felicia yanked a forgotten Skims number from the carnage, holding it up like Excalibur.

My eyes widened. "That's perfect!" Then I recoiled.

"Wait. This makes my ass look like a Georgia peach. He'll *know* I'm trying to seduce him." I flopped onto the bed, narrowly missing a rogue stiletto. "This is impossible. I'd rather file taxes in a hurricane."

Felicia tossed the dress at my face. "That's the point, you walnut. Seduce him! Monetize the Pilates!"

I groaned. "But it's too obvious! I'll look like I'm *trying*."

"You are trying! That's the entire plan!"

"No, the plan is to be subtly irresistible. Like… a mystery. A riddle wrapped in cashmere—not lycra."

Felicia stared at me. "You're overcomplicating this. Just wear the dress and bat your lashes like a siren."

I held it up again, scrutinizing my reflection. Okay, fine, my ass did look phenomenal. But if I paired it with a jacket—something casual, like "Oh, this old thing?"—and maybe didn't mention the 200 squats I'd done that week…

"Besides," Felicia added, "it's cooling off. You'll need a jacket anyway."

I narrowed my eyes. "Are you in on Lexi's scheme?"

"Obviously. I'm your hype man. Now *move*. You've got six minutes before you're late, and your eyeliner's wonkier than the last election."

Felicia sighed, and I caught the flicker of loneliness in her eyes—the kind that lingered like a houseplant everyone forgets to water. She'd mastered the art of the "totally fine" smile, but ever since Eric and I became a thing, that smile had started to crack at the edges, like a phone screen after a bad drop. I knew her well enough to recognize the quiet when's-my-turn? screaming behind her "casual" brunch stories about Tinder swipes named Brent who love hiking.

We'd both been single for years, but now I had Eric, and Felicia? Her love life was a rotating door of "Hey, stranger" texts and men who thought "meaningful relationships" meant being stuck in the talking stage for months. She swore it was enough, but we both knew her idea of romance wasn't a Netflix-and-chill with a side of "Don't text me tomorrow."

I'd once tried to play Cupid by suggesting Shane, our barista-slash-human-golden-retriever, since he shared her passion for sourdough and café gossip. She'd recoiled like I'd asked her to marry a toaster. "He's like a brother!" she'd hissed, as if I'd suggested they start a cult.

Now, guilt gnawed at me like a hangry Pomeranian. I wasn't responsible for her happiness, yet here I was, obsessing over her love life like it was an Insta story about to expire—while my own date with Eric was minutes away.

A knock at the door jolted me.

"Ohmygodhe'searly," I whisper-yelled, scrambling to check my phone. No texts. No warnings. Just betrayal. I spun to Felicia, eyes wild. "Can you get it? Please? I look like I've been attacked by a laundry hamper!"

She rolled her eyes so hard I heard them rattle. "Fine. But you owe me a day off."

She yanked open the door. "Oh. It's *you*," she said, flat as day-old Prosecco. "I thought it was my sushi."

Eric's voice rumbled through the apartment like velvet. "Hi, Felicia. Is Eva home?"

"Hi, Felicia. Is Eva home?" she mocked, voice tight. "Of course she is, where else would she be? She's been talking non-stop about your date—so it better be a good one."

Crap.

I glanced down at my outfit—Shein shorts with a mysterious stain, a T-shirt that read "I Paused My Game to Be Here", and hair that could double as a bird's nest. The Skims dress? Scrunched under a throw pillow somewhere.

Eric stood there, looking like he'd been airbrushed by a *GQ* intern—crisp shirt, tailored trousers, hair obeying the laws of physics. Meanwhile, I looked like I'd been dragged through a hedge by a raccoon.

Without hesitation, Eric strode in like he owned the

place (and, let's be honest, my sanity). In two steps, he closed the distance between us, wrapping me in one of those hugs that felt less "hello" and more "I'm claiming you for the mothership." Before I could squeak a protest, he hoisted me up like I weighed nothing. I melted like a popsicle in July, my limbs going rogue as I sank into his warmth, and caught the faint scent of his cologne.

My lips crashed into his—soft, insistent, familiar—while my fingers dove into his hair. For a blissful moment, my brain short-circuited. Outfit? Forgotten. Neuroses? Silenced. The fact that my T-shirt now read "I Paused My Game to Be Here" upside-down? Irrelevant.

"I'm not ready yet," I mumbled against his mouth as he set me down, my feet rebelling against gravity.

"Take all the time you need," he said, already drifting toward the kitchen like a man who'd never counted macros.

A few months ago, I'd have panicked about Felicia spilling my secrets—"Did you know Eva had a three-step-plan? Yeah, that blew up in her face."—but now? Eric belonged here, sandwiched between my chaos and Felicia's eye rolls, like a hot glue gun holding my life together.

I shut the bedroom door and slid down it like a rom-com cliché. *This is my life now.* Eric, the human forklift, showing up unannounced, kissing me like it's his job, and choosing me despite that one—*fine!* more than one—misunderstanding. And guess what? I *deserved* it.

My gaze snagged on the Skims dress, scrunched under a throw pillow. *Fine.* If gold-digging required weaponized *ass*ets, so be it.

I wriggled into the dress and faced the mirror. My ass looked like it had been sculpted by Michelangelo after a double espresso.

When I emerged, Eric's eyes darkened like storm clouds over a brunch reservation. His gaze raked over me, hot enough to melt the polar ice caps. A blush crept up my neck, but I leaned into it. Our relationship was still new enough to give me butterflies—and established enough to flutter lower ones.

I shook like a leaf walking to his car, a sleek black number parked illegally—neighbor's spot, obvs—but the ambiance changed when I slid in. Cool, collected, ice queen. *Gold-digging* ice queen.

He held my hand, his hand warm and cozy and... grounding. "Ready?"

Ice queen who? "Ready."

Felicia would've cackled. Lexi would've demanded he book a private jet to Napa. But tonight?

Tonight, as Eric yammered about the "cozy, intimate" restaurant he'd chosen (Translation: No Michelin stars), I let his voice fade into a hum. My heartbeat drowned out everything but the memory of his hands on my waist, his laugh against my ear, and the way he'd somehow turned my dumpster fire of a life into something resembling a rom-com montage.

Gold-digging could wait. Right now, I was too busy being stupidly, *recklessly* happy.

"Mind if I stop for gas?" Eric asked, already signaling. "Didn't want to be late, so I skipped it earlier."

"Of course not," I said, channeling my inner chill girlfriend—then immediately winced. Lexi's voice screeched in my head: "He's training you to accept mediocrity! Next he'll suggest splitting the bill at McDonald's!"

He pulled into the station, pumping a hurried $10 like he was defusing a bomb. "This'll do," he muttered, jaw tight, fingers drumming the nozzle. And that's when it hit me—Eric was nervous. Nervous! Mr. UFC, with his abs and his jawline and his ability to bench-press a Mini Cooper, was sweating this date.

I bit my lip to hide a grin.

Power shift: unlocked.

CHAPTER

SIX

TWENTY MINUTES LATER, WE arrived at a swanky off-Strip lounge—the kind where the menus don't have prices and the bread basket costs more than my phone bill. Lexi would've cooed, "Finally, a man who knows the difference between Prosecco and prison hooch."

"What are you drinking?" Eric asked, squinting at the wine list like it was a calculus exam.

"Rosé?" I said, before Lexi's voice hissed, "Champagne and nothing else, Eva!" My head shook like a bobblehead. "No, no. Champagne."

"Rosé champagne?" Eric suggested, grinning like he'd invented fire. "Two birds, one stone."

(Note: Two birds, one *gold digger*.)

He ordered a bottle of Armand Rosé with the casual

confidence of a man who'd never accidentally bought "Brut" thinking it meant "budget." I peeked at the menu—$300?!—and nearly inhaled my napkin. Lexi would've high-fived me. I, however, made a mental note to Venmo him $5 for solidarity.

As the bottle emptied (mostly into me), we chatted about nothing—his training, my "career" (a generous term for my café floundering/clinic helper), whether pineapple belongs on pizza (it *does*, fight me). The nerves dissolved, replaced by a warm buzz that had nothing to do with champagne.

Then he veered into dangerous territory.

The "modern women" talk.

Here we go, I thought, gripping my glass like a weapon. *Say something sexist, and I'll waterboard you with this $300 rosé.*

But Eric, bless his uncomplicated soul, said, "Chivalry's great, but it's a hit or miss with women nowadays."

I blinked.

He stumbled over his words. "I mean, solely in that a man's chivalry is not a life plan. A woman should never rely on some guy to fix your flat tire. Or your life."

Lexi's voice screeched again: "Abort! He's smarter than he looks! Told you to go for an oldie—they're a sure thing!"

"How many 'hits and misses' are we talking, exactly?" I teased, but we just laughed. I could hear Felicia chirping in, "Password share. That's a tell, Eva!" I continued, "Because my dad's idea of life skills was teaching me to call him when in need. Independence? Please. I'm one flat tire away from sobbing in a ditch."

Eric downed the last of his third old fashioned—because apparently UFC fighters metabolize alcohol like superheroes —and smirked. "You're plenty independent. You work, you pay bills, you *exist* without a man. A hundred years ago, they'd have burned you at the stake for that."

I sighed dramatically. "Sometimes I wish I could outsource my decisions. 'Alexa, pick a career path!' But yes, fine, teach my future daughter tires. *Got it*."

He grinned. "And oil changes. They're vital."

"Says the guy who probably owns a wrench collection. Hard pass. I'll stick to tires. And Googling 'how to scream for help politely.'"

Eric swirled his empty glass, then hit me with a smirk so cheeky I half-expected jazz hands. "But you're not *against* a guy holding doors, right? Or, say… showing up under your window with a boombox? *Say Anything* vibes?"

My eyes lit up. "*Yes!* "Molly Connolly" is my favorite."

His brow furrowed. "…Molly who?"

"'Molly Connolly.' From Say Anything?"

Eric blinked, then dragged a hand down his face like he was wiping off a bad Snapchat filter. "What are you on about?"

"What are *you* on about?!"

"The *movie*. John Cusack? Boombox? 'In your eyes…'" He hummed off-key, doing a little shoulder shimmy that should've been illegal.

I nearly snorted champagne out my nose. "Oh my god! You're talking about the *movie*? I thought you meant the *band*! How old are you, grandpa? Thirty?"

"Thirty-*three*," he said, leaning back with a grin. "You?"

"Twenty-eight. Which means I'm young enough to need subtitles for your ancient references."

The night spiraled from there—jokes, eye rolls, and a shared dessert I'm 90% sure was just an excuse to feed each other melted chocolate. The champagne was long gone, but the buzz? Still going strong.

I leaned in, lowering my voice like I was sharing state secrets. "Wanna go somewhere really cool?"

Eric raised a brow. "Define 'cool.' Is there a bed

involved? Because my bedtime's 10 p.m."

"Ten? Confirmed: you're a senior citizen. Do you need a nap? A prune smoothie?"

He laughed, and I gave his arm a playful punch—the kind that probably felt like a kitten swatting a brick wall to someone who bench-presses SUVs for fun.

"Where to?" he asked, still grinning like this was the most ridiculous adventure he'd ever signed up for.

"Mala Vida at the Sahara. Latin night. We'll salsa until our knees give out and drink until we forget our own names."

He'd never been, but when we stumbled onto the dance floor, it became painfully clear why. Eric moved like a robot programmed by a dad at a wedding—all stiff shoulders and cautious hip wiggles, as if his muscles had collectively agreed salsa was an OSHA violation. It was adorable, in a "baby giraffe learning to ice skate" sort of way.

But then the tequila shots kicked in.

The room began to spin like a disco ball dropped from a helicopter. The music melted into a fuzzy hum, and time dissolved into a puddle of off-beat dance moves and bad decisions. At some point, everything went black and I didn't get to call him an old man again.

The next morning, I woke up in a bed that screamed "IKEA showroom reject" – all grim gray sheets and a duvet that could double as a sketch pad. At least it had pillows. *Small mercies*, I thought, like I'd just survived a night in a Travelodge sauna. The walls were bare, and not a single rogue sock or half-dead succulent in sight.

(Translation: This is not my bed. Unless I've hired a *straight* man for interior decor.)

Panic hit me like a 6 a.m. Uber receipt email after a night out.

Fuck.

I jackknifed upright, heart doing the salsa. Shit. Shit. *Shit.*

A frantic pat-down confirmed two things:

1) I was still wearing the Skims nylon dress I'd agonized over for three hours last night.

2) My panties – tragic, greige Victoria Secret basics – were still firmly aboard the USS Carney.

The relief lasted exactly 1.2 seconds before the existential horror rebooted.

I tiptoed to the door, half-expecting a walk of shame

soundtracked by *Survivor* drums.

"Rise and shine, sleepyhead," came a voice as familiar as my 3 p.m. cortado addiction.

There stood Eric, holding a mug of coffee like some sort of caffeinated Prince Charming. Bastard. His hair was stupidly perfect – *how?* – and he'd clearly raided the "casually hot" section of the men's H&M. I bit back a grin. *If he has avocado toast in that kitchen, I might have to forgive him for looking so* fresh.

"Figured you'd need a cup," he said, sliding the mug over. "Two sugars, splash of milk. None of that non-fat-oat-milk-with-a-dash-of-cinnamon-pumpkin-latte you're used to."

I snorted. "Thanks."

"I'm making breakfast. I hope you're hungry."

The kitchen was aggressively *him*: all off-white walls and new-build cabinets. And there he was, flipping pancakes in those Dick Print sweats, like this was some sort of Calvin Klein ad. Abs glinting. Shoulders shouldering. And a tiny little scar under the left rib. I think. See, I wasn't quite sure, as I wasn't really looking.

Get a grip, you walnut! I told myself, sipping the coffee. Maybe, if he played his cards right, come Christmas he'll know I like my coffee iced. Alaska waterfall cold, just like the one I needed to dunk myself in right about now.

Shirtless Eric was a force—a dark force. He wasn't just tanned—he was *Baywatch* era Zach Efron levels of golden. The kind of tan that whispered, "I moisturize with SPF 5 with *gusto*." My gaze snagged on the scar under his ribs—a wonky little line—and the faint trail of hair that disappeared into his jeans. *Focus, Eva. Do not mentally Photoshop him into a Calvin Klein billboard.*

And there I was, legs dangling off a barstool like a kid waiting for a McDonald's Happy Meal, brain screaming: *Did we do it? Am I officially a walk of shame cliché?!*

The air crackled like a faulty toaster. *His* fault, obviously. Men shouldn't be allowed to exist shirtless before noon. It's unnatural. Illegal, even.

I blurted, "So, um. Last night. Did we… you know?"

His smirk could've powered the Strip. "Did we what?"

"Did we do it?" I whispered, hiding my face behind the coffee mug.

He chuckled. "No. You did try to pole dance using a lamppost, though." He paused. "Oh, and you licked my face."

Mortification hit me like a pre-made turkey sub to the

forehead. "I *what*?"

"Relax. I've had worse from my mom's spaniel." He stepped closer, all smug shoulders and crunches-for-fun energy. "Though you did call me Dick Print a few times."

My vision zoomed. "*Liar.*"

"Ask the bouncer. He recorded it for his TikTok."

I groaned into my hands. "Kill me. Bury me next to the Christmas returns collection."

His laugh was warm as a his coffee. "Relax. You're a fun drunk, and that's all I'm going to say." Then he kissed me—soft, lingering, *stupidly* good—and my brain short-circuited like a Temu hair straightener. "And a damn good dancer."

Fucking hell. Last night's regrets were rapidly being replaced by a new one: *not* jumping him like a half-price *Goop* candle.

CHAPTER

SEVEN

I BURRITO-ED MYSELF DEEPER into my coat—a Burlington puffer that had seen more winters than my love life—as the autumn air stabbed at me like a passive-aggressive CVS cashier. *Fucking hell, autumn's gone full Arctic winds*. After a summer that felt like Satan's armpit, this chill was jarring.

Lexi, meanwhile, lounged like a blue-blooded Fenty model in her lavender knit set—the one that probably cost more than Shane's monthly salary. The sweater was the exact shade of "I kill orchids for fun" and made her look almost approachable. *Almost*. Even after a 10-hour workday and Tegan's "disruptive skincare" PowerPoints, her blowout still defied gravity, posture straighter than a Palms Ghostbar vodka tonic.

"So," she drawled, swirling her margarita. "How long's

the drought been? Six months? A year?"

I slumped lower, hands over my face. "Two."

The squad erupted like I'd confessed to bumping uglies with a *Love Island* reject. Felicia snorted her margarita. *Traitor*.

"Two years?!" Lexi's gasp could've powered a trip to the moon. "Eva, even my cleaning lady's had more action—and she's a nun!"

"Hey! There was that *thing* with the guy from Pilates!" I lied, desperate.

Felicia—evil incarnate in Zara culottes – leaned in. "You mean *Tom*? The 'situationship'?" She air-quoted it like it was a dirty word. "Babe, that was before COVID."

Rude. I chucked a tortilla chip at her. "It was *late* 2021—"

"—And he still owes you for half that Chipotle's," Lexi cut in, cutting as a stray fish bone. "Babe, even I-sleep-at-8-on-the-dot-Charles texts his exes faster than your dry spell."

Charles. Her on-again-off-again TFMAM (Trust Fund Middle-Aged Man™). Two weeks ago, she'd been sulking because he'd "forgotten" her birthday (i.e.: sent roses instead of diamonds). Now that he'd booked a "surprise" Maldives trip (his assistant planned it), she was glowing like a Chanel ad. It was all, of course, a last-ditch attempt by the trust-funder to win back Lexi with all her good graces intact. Jury was still out, thought.

I squinted at her. "I don't think TFMAM Charles counts, actually."

"Does too," Lexi said, fluffing her hair to the side with practiced effortlessness. "He's old, not dead."

Bitter, I said, "Do you actually like him, or just his Amex?"

She sipped her drink, all innocence. "Why not both?"

Felicia fake-gagged. "You're both tragic. Eva's celibate, Lexi's dating a walking ATM—"

"—And you're dating *Tinder Plus*," Lexi shot back.

The bickering devolved, but I zoned out, crunching ice like it held life's answers. *Two years.* Jesus. At this rate, my next one would be sponsored by The Love Store clearance aisle.

Claire's head snapped up like meerkat spotting a Door Dash driver. "What Pilates guy?" she demanded, her voice sharp with curiosity.

I groaned louder than the honks at rush hour. *For Pete's sake.* We'd exhumed this corpse of a situationship more times than *Real Housewives* resurrected the New York cast. "You've known about him," I muttered, burrowing deeper into my

Costco blanket ($12.99, baby). "It's been two years. Let it rest, yeah?"

But Claire—manicured talon tapping her margarita glass like Morse code—was already doing mental math. "Wait, that was before I spawned Ethan, right?" She started counting months on fingers and kept going and *going*.

I shot Cali a "help me" look. She smirked into her virgin piña colada, the traitor.

"Fine!" I blurted, surrendering like a soggy sock. "It was that one-nighter turned six-month situationship. Worse than a DMV line on a walk-in day. I was miserable, but leaving felt like defusing a bomb in heels!"

The table erupted like a stripper cop just came in about a noise disturbance at a bachelorettes.

"Oh honey, that was *pre-COVID*!" Claire cackled, her "cool mom" persona slipping to reveal the demon beneath. Easy for her to judge—she'd gone from Tinder to car seats faster than I could say "condom split."

Cali—my actual flesh and blood—leaned in, all faux sympathy. "Poor Eric. Only guy in Vegas who hasn't navigated your I-15, huh?"

"Cali!" I threw a tortilla chip at her—with guac. "You're dead to me."

"Truth hurts, sis." She dodged, grinning like a villain. "Tick-tock, Eva! His DMs are fuller than a half-off buffet."

Lexi—perched like Cruella de Vil at a Dalmatian adoption—fixed me with that look. "Babe, he's not leaving you for Tegan. Unless she invents time travel *and* a personality."

I chugged my margarita. *Fucking hell.* Eric *had* shut Tegan down, but still—

"Oh. My. God." Felicia slammed her drink down, eyes wide as a sewer rat spotting an abandoned taco. "You're scared he'll ditch you after you smash! Like you're a midnight Taco Bell he'll swap for a 2-for-1 McDonald's!"

The table fell silent. Then—

"Oh my god, yes!" they chorused, clinking glasses like they'd cured cancer.

I slumped deeper into my blanket cocoon. Great. Now they'd cracked it—I was romantically constipated, and Eric was my emotional Imodium.

"What? No!" I squawked, voice cracking. "I'm just… building anticipation. Like Mariah Carey before Christmas time but with less whistles."

Claire's stare sharpened to Karen-from-HR levels. "Eva, babe, if you're not greedily eager to climb that man like the

Yosemite El Capitan, you need therapy. And not the bougie 'sound bath' kind—the 72-hour stay, Xanax-in-your-coffee therapy." She paused, faux-sweet. "Shall I book you in?"

"I *will* sleep with him!" I hissed, clutching my marg like a stress ball. "When I'm good and ready. When the stars align. When—"

Felicia snorted into her margarita with extra tequila. "At this rate, you'll be a born-again virgin—the Patron Saint of Blue Balls."

Bold words from someone whose 2020-present Tinder bio read "Life's short, let's make tonight memorable and split the tab."

Lexi glanced up from her phone—probably sexting Charles in emojis only bankers understand—and smirked. "*Born-again virgin*. Iconic. I have a doctor for that."

The coven cackled like hyenas at my expense.

Okay. Time to nuke this conversation.

"Fine," I barked, slamming my glass down. "I slept at his apartment last week."

The silence was louder than an ambulance.

Felicia's jaw dropped. "You said you didn't—"

"No! *God.* We just woke up in the same house. He made

breakfast in his Calvin Klein's. Like platonic cuddle buddies."

"*Platonic?*" Lexi hissed, leaning in. "Babe, even IKEA instructions aren't that confusing."

Claire fake-swooned. "Next you'll say he quoted *The Notebook* while feeding you strawberries—as friends!"

The cackle again. Only louder this time.

"He made me pancakes," I muttered. "And a nice little coffee."

Felicia gasped like I'd confessed to sleeping with Henry Cavill. "Homemade pancakes and coffee?! That's more intimate than sex!"

"Well, shit," said Lexi, texting furiously—probably live-updating Charles. "You're basically married."

I facepalmed. This was going on *forever. As long as you're making Eric wait*, a thought snuck in. *Might as well make it count.*

"We didn't *do it*," I insisted, though my grin was wider than an IHOP breakfast. "But Jesus—imagine Henry Cavill crossed with the nice guy from work. Now add pancakes."

The coven descended like seagulls on a dropped hot dog. Lexi—ever the connoisseur of romance—leaned in. "Babe, morning afters are my specialty. Charles once booked us a yacht because I 'forgot' my panties."

Felicia snorted. "I woke up in a Motel 6 with a man named Trevor who quoted Adam Sandler movies all night. The trauma."

"I," Lexi purred, "once made a man cry by not texting back. Full hysterics. It was great."

I sipped my marg, a smug smile curling my lips. "Well, it's not like that with us. He's sweet. Took me dancing, made me breakfast. I could swoon if I let myself."

Lexi toasted me. "Genius. Now he'll spend months wondering if he's done enough or if he has to up his game."

"I'm not working him," I said, convinced that little bit had been a concussion or something.

Felicia slammed her glass down. "Bullshit. You definitely felt his penis. Admit it!"

"I did not!"

"—Liar!" Claire crowed. "Your face is redder than a Peloton workout!"

I folded. "Fine! He wore the Dick Print sweats for breakfast, but I didn't touch, happy?!"

The table roared. Time for payback.

"Speaking of horror stories—" I grinned wolfishly, "—

Felicia had a one-nighter with a vampire last Valentine's. Bite marks. Black cape. The whole shebang."

Felicia's shriek could've shattered glass. "Eva! He was a *Goth*, you bitch!"

"He drank your *wine* and hissed at the sun! Left bites all over, too!"

Lexi doubled over. "Was his name Lestat? Dracula? *Edward?*"

The teasing devolved. Felicia hurled a chip. Claire live-imagined it. And just like that, Eric's Dick Print was old news.

Crisis averted. For now.

CHAPTER
EIGHT

☙

"YOU'RE DITCHING THE MORNINGS?" Cindy's eyebrow arched higher than the Stratosphere. "What's next —a yoga retreat during flu season?"

I'd finally mustered the courage to ask for a semi-adult gap year—or, as I'd pitched it, "strategic career diversification." (Translation: my tart crust could double as a doorstop.) With Dr. Rand off "finding himself" in Bali (i.e.: Instagramming avocado smoothies with pretty locals), the clinic was chaotic enough to make my request sound almost sensible.

"Just a month!" I chirped, ignoring the Everest of un-scanned files all over her desk. "I'll be back before you can say 'ER waiting times'!"

"I was counting on you for scanning these documents!"

"Rain check?"

Cindy sighed like I'd asked to convert the break room into a DJ tent at Coachella. "Fine. But if Claire 'forgets' her shifts one more time—"

"—You'll feed her to the printer. Understood."

"Told you small business ownership sucks" Lexi said when I dropped my new schedule. She'd quite literally never said that, but now that she'd shacked up with Tegan on a skincare line, maybe business *did* suck. "Should've snagged a banker like I suggested."

"You introduced me to Scott "Criminal and Fugitive" Van Hoff."

She shrugged like a porcupine shedding needles. "Same difference. At least Tegan *tried* gold-digging. Shame her target expired before the prenup."

The only thing Tegan's scandal had achieved was a million followers who live for drama thicker than a televised messy love triangle. Lexi swore their "brand synergy" could print money—if they could launch products faster than a DoorDasher in a Smart Car. Sadly, Tegan's backup plan—a sex tape so dull it made *Grace and Frankie* look X-rated— had tanked harder than the stock market on a downer.

(Translation: No one wanted to tune in to see Scott

getting the royal treatment. (Pegging, anyone?))

She'd never admit it, but we all knew Tegan had hoped to be the next Kim K, only to realize the market for "influencers getting pegged by retirees" was… *niche*. Turns out, the golden era of OnlyFans was so 2020. Even her viral meltdown ("Scott stole my Birkins—and my dignity!") couldn't revive her flatlining Venmo.

Hence Lexi's sudden devotion to Charles. Not that she'd make it easy—she'd made him jump through more hoops than an *American Idol* contestant on Red Bull. But he (his wallet) was persistent. It made him (his Amex) entirely irresistible to Lexi, especially now that she'd discovered what a nightmare startups were.

"Gold-digging's an art form," Lexi purred, scrolling through Charles' latest text—a diamond necklace link with a single word: "Yours?"

"It's a grift," I said, reorganizing appointment slots for the 10th time. "Even you can't Netflix-and-chill your way into generational wealth."

She smirked, all predator-in-Prada. "Babe, I don't chill. I marinate."

I snorted. "You're marinating Charles into an early grave. Just marry him already—he's practically given you half his net worth, might as well make it 100%."

"Patience." She sipped her $15 green juice, courtesy of Charles' Uber Eats delivery. "Once he transfers Scott's offshore millions to *my* account, I'll consider a chapel. Maybe."

"Delusional."

"Manifesting." She winked. "Once I'm loaded, I'll bankroll your bakery. You'll name a croissant after me."

"Call it the Gold Digger Deluxe," I muttered. "Filled with hollow promises and edible glitter."

"Perf."

I slumped deeper into my chair, all this easy money talk giving me the jitters. "Babe, it's a dumpster fire. And the worst bit? I never wanted to be Candace Nelson! Felicia *volun-told* me into this disaster."

Let's be clear: the café wasn't losing money. Mostly because it became a UFC-level spectacle after The Incident™ (i.e.: the misunderstanding of a lifetime à la *Celebrity Deathmatch*, only Eric was the only celebrity). Tourists now flocked in like pigeons to Desert Bloom Café, desperate to see "where the chaos happened."

Oh, and Eric's UFC buddies had adopted the place as their second home. Which meant daily sightings of men built like brick saunas, grunting over oat lattes and protein smoothies. Their fanbase was mostly men who thought "tap out" was a personality trait… and a shockingly large number of women who "don't usually watch UFC, but wow, is he single?"

Very. Ripped. Brick. Saunas. Chick magnets, if you will.

Lexi tossed a stress ball at me. "Tell Felicia you're out! Let her take out a loan—or better yet, sell the place to Starbucks. They'll put in millions, pay off your debt, problem solved."

She'd been nagging me for weeks to ditch Felicia's businesswoman plan for me, and *god*, some days I wanted to. But then I'd catch Felicia grinning like she'd won *The Great British Baking Show* just because someone ordered a tart, and… ugh. My resolve melted into a puddle of tears and lost wishes.

Plus, she viewed the café as my "repayment" for being her unpaid Uber during her "crisis era" (i.e.: two years of ferrying her to and from work, picking her up after a Tinder swipe left mid-date, the works). Hard to argue semantics when she's got receipts—and a guilt trip sharper than a slap on the cheek.

"I can't," I groaned, refreshing the appointment system like it'd cure my ennui—and my uncertainty.

Truth was, I hated my day job too. But quitting felt like swapping one soggy sock for another. Felicia, though? She'd torch her life for the chance—walked out of a law career, her parents' group chat, everything—just to chase this half-baked dream.

"She's happy," I mumbled. "Like, Disney princess happy."

Lexi rolled her eyes. "And you're Happy Meal happy. Temporarily amused, deeply unfulfilled. You're spread thinner than jam on toast, babe. Fix it before you end up on *Dr. Phil* sobbing into a Dyson."

She paused, faux-thoughtful. "Or... bag that UFC moneybag. Get him to fund your real passion—watching *Pride and Prejudice* and *The Notebook* on repeat. Pilates membership included."

I snorted loud enough to startle a patient in the waiting room.

"Lexi—"

"What? He's already husband material—just a little spice and a no prenup non-negotiable."

"Oh god, I couldn't do as much as sneeze at that, let alone hint."

She shrugged, as if saying "must not want it enough, you

walnut." "So, how's it going with Mr. Dick Print anyway?"

I bit back a grin to our old nickname for Eric. "Slow. Excruciatingly slow. Like, I-15 to California on the weekend slow."

Lexi's smirk could've cut diamonds. "For someone who claims she's 'not playing games,' you're running circles around him. *Love Island* contestants could never."

I frowned. "What're you on about?"

"You're making him *wait*, babe. Most girls these days hand over the goods faster than a drive-thru order on a Friday. But you? You're the Hermès of women—luxury, limited stock, membership required—and most important, a sizable investment."

"I'm *not* a gold digger," I protested, though I snorted into my iced tea brew. Truth was, I didn't know the first thing about scheming—unless you counted my failed attempt to three-step my way into the VIP server lifestyle. But Eric? I liked him. *Really* liked him. My heart even did a salsa routine every time he texted.

"Sure," Lexi drawled, filing her nails. "But go on—what's he bought you?"

I hesitated, suddenly wanting to please her. "He... ordered a bottle of Armand the other night."

Her eyebrows hit her hairline. "Ace of Spades. Fitting. Keep this up, he'll be signing his house over by Christmas."

"Lexi—"

"What? Men love a challenge! Next he'll be buying you a Chanel just to get a kiss."

I buried my face in my hands. "I nearly fainted when I saw the bill the other night. I'm not cut out for your gold digger act."

She stood, slinging her stethoscope like a weapon. "Listen—you're the *Tiffany's* of this relationship. He's the Ross tea set. Act like it."

As she strutted off, I texted Felicia: "Got mornings free now. Let's *not* burn the café down."

Her reply was a hurried: "Thank god. New barista quit after mistaking salt for sugar. Again."

I stared at my phone, feeling that too-familiar sense of sinking. Great.

Lexi's voice echoed in my head: "You're the prize, babe."

And okay, fine—maybe her "grind him down until he buys you a penthouse next to mine" ethos was… slightly less deranged than I'd thought. Or maybe, I was up to here in problems. It wasn't my intention, but every day and in every way, Lexi's gold digging ideology seemed less and less unethical.

CHAPTER

NINE

THEY SAY BEHIND EVERY great man is a woman rolling her eyes and muttering, "I taught him that." No brothers to test the theory on, but Eric? Living proof.

The man wasn't just a "nice guy," he was the Whole Foods of men: wholesome, ethically sourced, suspiciously perfect. No "I'm a feminist, but…" vibes. Just pure "make tampons tax-free" energy.

Raised on proper mac and cheese —actual cheddar, not that neon powder muck—and meatloaf Mondays his mom batch-cooked between nursing shifts. The woman was a legend. And with my own mother's mantra swimming in my mind—"Watch how he treats his mom. That's your future, sweetie."—I was safe. If true, I'd hit the jackpot. The man folded laundry *and* remembered her birthday.

Lexi would sneer, "Mama's boy alert!" but come on—the woman lived in Michigan. If she'd stopped him moving to Vegas to punch people for cash, *then* we'd chat. But no—she'd taken him to karate since he was in diapers. Obviously he'd end up a UFC champion, with bragging rights, too.

We'd orbited the same city for years, yet only collided once fate—or sheer desperation—plonked his gym next to my accidental café. Coincidence? Please. This was "written in the stars" levels of engineered. Couldn't have pulled it off if we'd tried.

Had we met in my "Tegan stole my job and my boyfriend" era? He'd have fled faster than a bat from drizzle. And his "party hardy" phase? Hard pass. I've seen his Myspace. *Shudder.*

But now here he was, shirtless (not really, I only wished) in my kitchen, whisking noodles like Martha Stewart after a martini.

Timing, babe. It's not just for Spirit flights.

Eric asked about my family more than the DMV asks for proof of address. Forgotten what it felt like, honestly—a man listening? Not just waiting for his turn to talk about his fantasy football league? Revolutionary.

For years, I'd assumed all relationships were doomed to pull a *Titanic*—thanks, ex who ran off with Tegan like she was the last lifeboat. But Eric was more Smokey Bear than *Wolf of Wall Street*. Patient. Kind. Shockingly uninterested in pressuring me into anything—sex, speed-drying mascara, or merging onto the I-15 at rush hour.

Lexi's voice haunted me: "Men want one thing, babe. Make 'em pay for it." But Eric broke the mold—probably with those UFC hands. Here I was, a certified gold-digger-in-training, suddenly struck useless by a man who brought me tea before I'd even fake-sneezed.

Pathetic.

I was gone. Brain like a broken record:

Eric. Fucking. Mann. On repeat.

We spent evenings in his kitchen—him cooking actual food, me perched on the counter like a confused meerkat.

"Sis does the best buttered noodles," he said, stirring a pot like a witch at a cauldron.

I eyed the gloop. "This is your secret weapon? Carbs and… butter?"

"Family recipe." He grinned, all dimples and delusion. "Comfort food."

Comfort? Looked like something Olive Garden would reject, but I'd have licked the bowl for that smile.

Then a plan began forming in the back of my mind, dusting places left alone too long. *Surprise him with a family reunion! Fly his Michigan mom over, maybe a sibling or two.* Girlfriend kind of stuff.

Wait—girlfriend? Me? Since when did I morph into the *Notting Hill* poster girl?

But as he talked about his sister's noodle triumphs, eyes all soft-focus Henry Cavill, I realized that no, it wasn't hard. Kinda natural, actually.

Harder than explaining *Love Is Blind* to his mom, though.

He dolloped a coronary's worth of butter into the pan, followed by a snowfall of sawdust Parmesan that could double as snow. Licking the spoon like a man who'd never heard of salmonella, he tossed it back into the gloop with the confidence of a professional. Mesmerizing. The man moved through life like a TikTok ASMR video—no stress, just *vibes.*

"Taste," he ordered, shoving the spoon at me.

I licked it. Jesus. Pure carbed-up nostalgia. "Holy hell, that's good."

He smirked, stirring like a *Hells Kitchen* pro. "You hate buttered noodles? Sis and I survived on these. Student budget cuisine."

I snorted. We might as well have been raised on different

planets. My childhood smelled of chipotle and lime, not Ikea meatballs. "Babe, I'm Mexican. Our comfort food's got more kick than airplane disturbance."

"That's only 'cause you haven't had mine," he teased, grin wider than a CVS receipt.

That flutter again. The one that felt like a Thursday salsa routine in my ribs. "I grew up on *fajitas*, not butter carb specials. Your noodles don't stand a chance."

His eyes lit up like I'd mentioned a secret Chipotle menu. "Fajitas? Cook those for me sometime?"

"Fine, but they're not *Taco Bell*," I warned, but he was already closing in, spoon abandoned, lips quirking.

"Even better." His kiss tasted like butter and excitement. I melted faster than a Magnum in a heatwave.

"Let's do a weekend away," he murmured, all low tones and pent up intensity. "Just us. No UFC, no café fires. No cackle-y friends."

Panic flashed—what if I snore? What if he's a secret sock-to-bed-wearer?—but Lexi's voice hissed, "Take chances, Eva! Or someone else will snatch him up faster than you can say penny digger."

"That sounds lovely." I sighed, lovey-dovey and everything sappy. "But if you hate my *sopita*, I'm blaming your Midwestern palate."

He laughed, stirring his noodles. "Speaking of—what's *sopita*?"

I leaned in, whispering like it was a state secret: "Angel pasta in tomato broth. You'll weep. Then propose."

Later, when the butter noodles were gone and half the day spent, the *fideo* hissed in the pan like a disgruntled Uber passenger, while Eric loomed over my shoulder like a *Hells Kitchen* judge with better abs.

"It's meant to sound like that," I said, stirring like my life depended on it. Mom's recipe was sacred—screw this up, and I'd be disowned faster than I could say "one more chance!"

Eric squinted at the sizzle. "You sure it's not burning?"

"Positive. Burnt *fideo's* what we want. Sort of." I shoved the spoon at him. "Stir that. Channel your inner Jamie Oliver."

He obeyed, brow furrowed like he was defusing a bomb, not angel hair pasta. Meanwhile, I blitzed tomatoes, garlic, and onion in the blender just like mom taught me.

The sauce hit the pan, and the smell was instant heaven. Or at least, a Chipotle's candle.

Eric's nostrils flared like he'd sniffed a truffle. "Holy hell.

That's… amazing."

"Told you," I preened, ignoring the doubt.

We fell into banter as the *sopita* bubbled—him teasing me about my *"MasterChef* delusions," me mocking his Midwestern palate ("You think mayo's spicy, babe"). Perched on the counter, I swung my legs, our shoulders brushing.

Then he stepped closer, hands landing on my hips like he'd claimed squatter's rights. His lips grazed my neck, voice a low rumble: "Let's go away for a weekend. Just us."

"Where?" I played coy, fingers in his hair—softer than my Costco throw.

"Anywhere." His grin was pure mischief. "Even Ikea, at this point."

I snorted. "What about Paris?"

"Paris?" He paused. "Casino Paris or *actual* Paris?"

I frowned, faking. "Whatever's in your budget, babe."

"Ikea it is."

We laughed, kissed.

He scooped me up, carrying me halfway out. "Let's go now," he grinned, all UFC arms and steel abs.

I squawked, flailing like a startled pigeon. "Eric—my

sopita's gonna char to a crisp!"

"Leave it," he declared, swinging me around like we were in a Richard Curtis montage. "We'll buy new pans in Paris. Eat pastries. Sip Hotel Chocolat sludge and croissants."

"Eric, that's hot chocolate, not Béchamel—put me down!"

He relented, setting me on the counter with a smirk that screamed all his feelings and it said "I'm falling for you" even if he didn't actually say it. "Eva. I'd take you anywhere if you asked. *Do* anything you wanted."

My chest thumped. "Alright, Romeo," I muttered, cheeks hotter than an extra hot jalapeño. "I believe you."

And just like that—*click*—the penny dropped. Lexi's voice cackled in my head: "You've bagged a banker, babe. Milk him like a California cow." Felicia's echoed: "Get that location share! Passwords, too! Gotta check it all. The DMs must be *wild*."

And my own thoughts saying he was *mine*. Passwords, salary, *inheritance*—all mine for the taking. I could've asked for a monthly allowance like Lexi said or a lifetime supply of 3 a.m. tacos. But no. All I wanted was kisses and smiles and *sweetness*.

"A weekend away, then," I said, voice wobbling.

"Perfect," he vowed, kissing me with the focus of a man who'd been made to wait for it. The world dissolved—no burnt noodles, no friendly advice, just his hands on my hips and my brain short-circuiting like a discount hairdryer.

"Don't care where," I lied. (*Please god, not a Travelodge.*)

"Only the best for you," he murmured, lips grazing my neck.

And there it was—the power. Lexi's gold-digger gospel rang in my ears. I could've drained his account, but instead I… hugged him back.

Pathetic.

But as his arms tightened, I let myself revel in it. Eric Mann: human golden retriever, UFC champ, my personal Snuggie blanket.

And he was all in.

CHAPTER

TEN

❧

"YOU MEAN YOU'RE STAYCATION-ING, not vacation-ing," Felicia snapped, flour flying like confetti at a *Survivor* finale. She was attempting to teach me pastry—a "simple" task, apparently, though my dough currently resembled Red Rock mud. "The Cosmopolitan isn't the Maldives, Eva. It's a Travelodge with a champagne menu."

I grimaced, clumsily hacking butter into chunks. "It's romantic, Fel. And I'm nervous, okay? We haven't even… you know. Longest time I've spent with him, I was blackout drunk."

"Egg. Now," she barked, Martha Stewart on a sugar crash. I dropped it in, yolk wobbling accusingly.

"Like this?" It'd been my seventh failure in as many days, and I wanted to get it right.

She nodded. "Maybe—" she sieged the dough like Gordon Ramsay spotting a mouse, "—you're scared he'll do a Tegan 2.0. Run off with some Insta baddie and leave you after taking your celibacy cherry. Understandable."

I froze. *Bingo.* "It's not just Tegan. He's UFC, Felicia. Women slide into his DMs like the Strip commuters at rush hour. I can't compete with that. I don't *want* to compete with that."

She snorted. "So hire a hitman. Or—" she brandished a rolling pin, "—lean into the crazy. Show up at his next fight in a 'Hands Off My Man' tee. Go full pre-*Snapped*."

I choked out a laugh. "Murder's illegal, babe. And kind of off-putting."

"Allegedly." She eyed my dough with disdain. "Jesus, Eva. This isn't pastry—it's cork board."

"You try being a newbie!" I gestured wildly, flinging flour onto the tea towels. "Not all of us were born with a whisk in hand!"

"Focus." She shoved the tart tin at me. "If you're this scared, why go?"

I hesitated. "...Because he remembers how I take my coffee. And he *listens*. Even when I rant about nothing at all."

Felicia's stern facade cracked. "Ugh. Disgusting." She

flicked dough at me. "Fine. But if you bail, I'm selling your *sopita* recipe to Chipotle."

"Not disgusting," I countered. "*Adorable*."

She leaned against the counter, eyeing my dough like it might do her in. "Look, babe—he's a UFC Dick Print with abs that could grate cheese. Of course girls are sliding into his DMs left and right. But you've got him on hold, which is genius. Bet he'd hand over his PIN faster than a Usain Bolt 100-meter dash if you asked. Check his Insta. Make sure he's not liking thirst traps. *Then* bang him senseless."

I flattened the dough with unnecessary violence. "I'm not his probation officer, Felicia. If he's a dirtbag, I'll find out when he forgets my birthday for a a Raya model. Until that happens—it won't, by the way!—I'll just chill."

She threw her hands up. "Fine! But don't stress about climbing him like a tree and *not* climbing him like a tree. Just do your post-divorce Adele redemption arc. And don't say I didn't tell you so."

Her advice haunted me all day. By 3 p.m., fueled by a break

room coffee and delusion, I strutted through the office like I'd invented sliced bread—shoulders back, hips swinging, radiating main character energy.

Reina—Claire's call out backup—squinted at me from her desk. "Your aura's glowing. Did you sage today?"

"Nope. Just dropped the bullshit and reminded myself to enjoy my day."

"Good for you," she said, singing along to Jason Aldean.

Lexi didn't glance up from her phone when I slumped next to her, she just said, "Heard about your staycation plans. The *Cosmopolitan*? Babe, if you're not upgrading to The Ritz, at least swipe the towels." She refreshed her screen and groaned.

"*And* the sample bottles," I muttered, floating back to my desk.

A month into Lexi and Tegan's "skincare empire" (i.e.: money grab serums and pocket change creams), Lexi "quit" our medical office job—for approximately 14 hours. She stormed back, claiming she "missed the banter" (Translation: Tegan's leaked sex tape flopped harder than a *Love Island* proposal, and their "business" was hemorrhaging cash faster than Charles' trust fund).

The tea, and only real explanation, was that Tegan's

OnlyFans "debut" earned less than a Starbuck's barista's hourly wage—in total. Their Instagram followers (1.2M thirsty bots, 200 actual humans) bought precisely *zero* clicks of Naked & Pegging by Tegan™. Fine, more than zero, but not by much. Lexi, ever the delusional queen, blamed streaming services for the fumble (i.e.: illegal downloads, like it was Y2K all over again). Presumably, Tegan's venture into Adult Entertainment 101 would've bagged more bills if she'd only teased an underboob, but since she'd introduced Scott Van Hoff's Star Spangled Starfish early on in the clip, the clicks had been null and void—zilch.

Of course, she done it with exclusive rights in mind—her own.

But let's be real—Lexi stayed at the office for the drama. Charles, her TFMAM, bankrolled her Tiffany's habit, but our office was her *stage*. Where else could she show off her Kelly like she was Carrie after a fight with Big? Nowhere else, that's where. She could quit and live off Charles' Amex, lounging in Bali with a Pilates instructor named Sven, but no. Lexi thrived on the illusion of independence, even if her paycheck barely covered her monthly dry-cleaning bill for sequined blazers.

Felicia insisted Lexi's work ethic came from her mom—a "generational grind" forged in 90s strip clubs. I reckoned Lexi just loved the thrill of almost getting caught scrolling

Chanel Official Website during flu season.

Meanwhile, Tegan's accounts were drier than an Outback steak. Scott's dodgy crypto schemes left her drowning in debt, and her new "Wellness Warrior" rebrand wasn't fooling anyone. Lexi's take was "Once a WAG, always a WAG."

Tegan's current hustle was speed-dating high net worth tourists who thought "hedge fund" was a personality, flirting with reality TV has beens from early 2010's and casually dropping "my ex, Scott Van Hoff…" like a hand grenade at the Ghostbar.

"Men are morons," Lexi declared, filing her nails. "They see another man's sloppy seconds and think 'Mmm, vintage.'"

She wasn't wrong. Tegan's DMs now included a rom-com has-been and a well-known politician with a very suspicious "yacht party" invite. Lexi was already drafting her resignation letter—pending Tegan's next nuptials.

But in true Vegas fashion? By tomorrow, the entire plan could implode.

All I wanted was a quiet life—one job, one Zara order a month, maybe a Hawaii timeshare if I felt spicy. But Lexi, ever the picture of ambition, thought my dreams were as small as a 2-for-1 Taco Bell deal.

"How do you know about the trip?" I groaned, already dreading the answer.

"Felicia spilled the beans. Also called you a 'repressed nun' but don't worry—" Lexi waved her phone, smirking like a siren, "—your secrets die with me. Mostly."

"I don't even get you anymore," I muttered. Was it me, or had her gold-digger manifesto started leaking into everything? "Ooh, Eva, steal his Rolex!" "Eva, his Amex is right there!"

"Step one: stop being a born-again virgin," she said, inspecting her nails. "It's a give and take, and babe, you gotta do some giving to do some taking."

"Maybe this weekend's the time!" I snapped, then cringed at my own defensiveness. Mocking friends was a sport—until you became the half-price champagne punchline.

"Oh! So the 'vaginal atrophy' era's over?"

"The *what?*"

"Felicia's words, not mine!" Lexi cackled, loud and annoying as hell. "Relax. Claire thinks you've got performance anxiety. I think you're just *rusty*."

"I'm never telling you guys *anything* again," I lied, laughter betraying me. Pathetic—I cared what they thought.

If the roles were reversed, I'd roast them into the Grand Canyon.

"Poor Eric," I sighed, "if he knew you two were sportsbooks betting on our sex life…"

"Poor Eric?" Lexi scoffed. "The man's a UFC beefcake in Dick Print sweats. He's got a small country's population in his DMs! Only "poor Eric" here is your fanny's stage fright."

Heat flooded my cheeks. Of course, she noticed.

"Lexi—"

"What?" She hip-checked me, grinning like "difficult" was her personality. "He's crazy for you. Just unclench, yeah? Let it happen. Naturally. Like an In-N-Out drive-thru. Slow and steady."

For a split second, through the sarcasm, it almost sounded like… sincerity.

Then: "But first, go drain his bank account. Gently."

"Easy peasy," I deadpanned.

Spoiler: It wasn't.

CHAPTER

ELEVEN

⌒

THE LAS VEGAS STRIP sprawled beneath me like a glittering disco ball dropped onto the desert. From our 45th-floor suite, I half-expected to see tiny Elvis impersonators waving from the rooftops, but no. My Chanel purse—last summer's "your net worth is showing" consolation price from Lexi after we stalked Tegan—slid precariously across the glass table. *Why do hotels insist on furniture that defies gravity?* I wondered, nudging it away from the edge before it could plunge to its death. Lexi claimed high-rise living was "aspirational," but all I felt was the ominous sway of a building that clearly missed its calling as a metronome.

Eric had vanished to hunt for ice, which was either adorably chivalrous or a thinly veiled excuse to pace the hallway muttering, "Don't screw this up, bud." Meanwhile, I was sweating all the little things.

I'd packed for this trip with the precision of a woman who'd watched *10 Things to Pack for a Hot Girl Summer!* at 2 a.m. Spoiler: My "capsule wardrobe" now consisted of three bikinis, a sarong that doubled as a picnic blanket, and a pair of mule heels so impractical they could double as murder weapons.

Why hadn't I brought actual clothes?

Felicia's voice rang in my head: "You'll regret it. But I won't care. I'll be too busy at Zara."

I eyed the bikini laid out on the bed. Right. Time to embrace the "confidence" chapter of that self-help book I'd abandoned. But as I tugged it on, I realized the "ruched" design wasn't "figure-flattering"—it was "sausage-casing chic." *Great.* Eric would either declare his undying love or mistake me for a Costco chicken bake.

Lexi's gold-digging commandments echoed in my mind: "Arch your back like you're in a *Little Mermaid* contests for best rock wave! Laugh at his jokes—even the unfunny ones! Casually mention you've always wanted a Kelly, just like me!" Exhausting. How did Tegan manage it? Oh, right—she'd constantly "accidentally" leave a Tiffany's tab open on Charles' laptop. Romance!

Lexi had trained me like a tiny, sequin-clad Napoleon, her battle cry echoing in my brain: "Make him spend, Eva!

It's not gold-digging—it's *strategic asset allocation*." Which, let's be real, was just a fancy way of saying "bleed him dry, but make it his idea."

She insisted my "celibacy pact" was genius—keeping Eric dangling like a piñata stuffed with cash. "Men love the chase, babe! The longer you withhold, the bigger the diamond!" Meanwhile, Eric, bless his oblivious heart, was out here dropping stacks on a Cosmopolitan suite because "the pool has sand, babe. It's basically Bora Bora, and didn't we want a little staycation?" Clueless. Completely clueless.

Felicia, of course, was Team "Jump His Bones Already." "Life's short, Eva! You're over here playing 4D chess while he's just... hot. And shirtless. And sweaty!" She'd text me eggplant emojis hourly, like a horny motivational coach.

Torn between Lexi's "monetize your mystique" hustle and Felicia's "screw his brains out" chaos, I did the only sane thing: I called my sister.

Cali, the human equivalent of a weighted blanket, answered on the first ring. "You're spiraling, aren't you?"

I word-vomited the whole saga—Lexi's spreadsheet of "investment milestones," Felicia's "sex now, panic later" agenda, Eric's baffling belief that a chlorinated puddle qualified as a "beach."

Cali sighed, the sound of someone who'd survived both

middle school *and* my teenage goth phase. "Eva. Breathe. Your instincts survived that guy who thought 'vegan' meant 'eats grass.' Trust them."

She bulldozed Lexi's "financial foreplay" nonsense and Felicia's "YOLO" anthem with three sentences: "If you wanna kiss him, kiss him. If you wanna buy yourself a spa day with his Amex, do that. Just stop treating your heart like a stock portfolio."

It was like she'd hosed down the dumpster fire in my brain. "Love isn't a Ponzi scheme, babe," she'd said. "And Eric's not a crypto bro—stop overcomplicating it."

So I hung up, poured a glass of wine, and texted Eric: "Beach's fake, but you're cute. Let's go!"

Lexi would've fainted. Felicia would've cheered.

But Cali? She'd just say: "See? Instincts. They're fine. Now go eat a snack and take a nap."

Poor Eric was blissfully unaware of the tsunami of overthinking crashing through my brain—or that my friends had mentally cast him in roles ranging from "suspiciously perfect" (Felicia) to "human cash machine" (Lexi, obvi). But Cali was right: the man had chosen me, a woman whose greatest luxury was remembering to spring clean on time. That had to count for something.

I flopped onto the bed, staring at the ceiling, and practiced serenity—or at least, not hyperventilating—until Eric returned with the ice bucket. And if ice was any indicator of the type of man Eric was, it would say he was a provider, because provide he did.

The door clicked open. Eric stood there, ice bucket in hand, looking like a *GQ* model who'd stumbled into a rom-com. *Deep breath, Eva. You've got this. Or at least, you've got a bikini up your* crack.

"Alright?" he said, grinning.

"Never better," I chirped, yanking the sarong over my hips like a Victorian ghost.

"Planning to ice-sculpt the Eiffel Tower?" I asked, eyeing the frosty mountain.

"Just… wanted to be prepared," he said, cheeks pinker than a Victoria Secret's Valentine's display.

The bucket was overflowing, and Eric was noticeably nervous and I finally relaxed because we were just two nervous people trying to start something real. In the end, half the ice was thrown out because the champagne bottle didn't fit and we'd had a good laugh, but at least the overflowing ice had broken the proverbial ice and all was well.

By the pool, I'd opted for my "practical" bikini—a term

meaning "covers 60% of my insecurities, 0% of my ass dimples"—while Eric's swim shorts screamed "I work out for a living!" We clinked our cocktails (mine was 80% pineapple, 20% courage) and wobbled into the water like over-caffeinated otters.

And you know what? Cali was right. Love *did* come naturally—or at least, splashing Eric while pretending to "accidentally" lose my bikini top did. (Spoiler: It stayed firmly tied. This time.)

As the sun dipped, painting the Strip in hues of pretty pink and pale blues, we trudged back to the room, damp and giggling, only to find the champagne still languishing in its icy grave. The bed loomed like a judgmental parent. *Deep breaths, Eva.*

But then Eric leaned in, his whisper tickling my ear: "Today was… perfect." Not "sexy." Not "life-changing." *Perfect.* And just like that, my nerves dissolved like sugar in a mojito.

By bedtime, I was glowing—half from the sun, half from residual panic—and slathered in enough aloe vera to qualify as a spa treatment. I emerged from the bathroom, expecting Eric to be snoring like a tractor, but no—there he was, shirtless and *awake*, wrestling with the blackout curtains like they'd block out his nerves too.

"Thought you might want privacy," he said, as the final drape fell, shielding us from the Vegas glow.

Oh? And there it was. No grand gestures, no diamond-encrusted Kellys—just a man who noticed things. *My* things.

"Thank you," I mumbled, heart in my throat.

"You can take the bed," Eric said, still fiddling with the curtains like they were a Rubik's Cube he was determined to solve. He was nervous—I could tell. The man was practically vibrating with "don't screw this up" energy. It was cute, actually, his nerves.

A sudden wave of boldness hit me—probably the champagne, or maybe the residual glow of my fresh tan giving me confidence. Before I could overthink it, I let my hotel robe slide off my shoulders, landing in a heap at my feet. *Subtle, Eva. Real subtle.*

He finally turned, his eyes locking onto mine, and for a split second, I wished I'd faced the other way. My Georgia peach ass was my good side, after all—my soft tummy, less so. But it was too late for strategic posing now.

"Maybe you can take the bed," I said, my voice softer than a throaty whisper.

He stepped closer, his breath shaky. "I've thought about this for so long," he whispered, and something inside me snapped. Not in panic, not in doubt—just pure, unadulterated *surrender*.

All the advice—Lexi's gold-digging commandments, Felicia's "just do him already!" nudges, Cali's "love is natural" pep talks—faded into the background. This wasn't about them or doubts or plans. This was about me. And Eric. And a bed that was definitely not big enough for all my overthinking.

We kissed, and he tasted of champagne and tiny tremors. We fell into bed, and it wasn't planned or strategic or even remotely sophisticated. It was natural and not one bit calculating. And love did come. Three times.

The next morning, I woke up feeling like I'd been dipped in sunlight and my body felt loved and *alive*. Eric was beside me, his hair adorably mussed, his arm slung over my waist like he'd done it a thousand times before.

"Wanna spend all day in bed?" he mumbled, his voice gravelly with sleep.

I laughed and bumped him and snuggled him like I'd done it for years. "No. I want to go back to the pool, get sunburned, come back, order room service, and drink champagne all day."

He kissed my shoulder, his lips warm against my skin. "Whatever you say."

Later, as a fresh bottle of champagne arrived and we lounged in a tangle of sheets and sunscreen, I leaned back against the pillows and thought: *Staycations? Underrated. Eric Mann? Overqualified.*

CHAPTER

TWELVE

"YOU'RE DOING IT WRONG again, Eva," Felicia snapped, flour dusting her eyebrows like she'd face-planted into a snowdrift. "This isn't rocket science. It's *shortcrust pastry*."

The café kitchen hummed with the gentle angst of Lauryn Hill's "Killing Me Softly"—or maybe that was just my internal soundtrack. Felicia had turned the music down to a funeral dirge, probably to avoid "distracting my creative process" (translation: drowning out my excuses—and my patience). The ovens had been blasting heat for hours, and at this rate, we'd single-handedly fund the power company's Christmas party.

I glared at the dough, which resembled a deflated football. "I weighed the butter! I sifted the flour! I even talked to the eggs!"

"Did you *chill* the dough?" Felicia demanded, wielding a rolling pin like a sword.

"I *glared* at it. Isn't that the same thing?"

She groaned. "Eva, you can't 'manifest' pastry. This isn't a mindfulness retreat. It's a *bakery*. And with all these failures, we're hemorrhaging!"

My eyes itched from exhaustion (and possibly flour-induced conjunctivitis). No amount of Eric's "stress relief techniques" (i.e.: last night's… *ahem*… four-round stress relief with Eric. Though, credit where it's due: the man could disassemble a bed frame faster than IKEA instructions) had prepared me for this. Not even his patented "Swedish massage" (which, let's be honest, was just him massaging my ass) could deal.

Felicia cranked up Lauryn Hill, possibly hoping divine intervention would strike. Instead, I exploded.

"Maybe I'm just not a baker, Felicia! Maybe I'm a… a pastry anarchist! A croissant heretic! Did you ever think of that?!"

She paused, a glob of dough stuck to her cheek. "Are you having a midlife crisis? Because I'm not paying for your pottery classes—in dough!"

"Did you ever think I can't bake, I can't make coffee, I

can't man the register. I can't do it because it's *not* what I want to do?!"

She sobered, face serious as a coronary. "I didn't force you to be here. And maybe you shouldn't be."

I gasped, stunned into silence. "You're firing me?"

"I'm considering it," she said, attacking the dough with renewed vigor. "You turned the mixer to 'tsunami' setting last week. Shane thinks you're a mole for *Starbucks*."

I slumped against the counter, a human puff pastry. "I just… wanted to help."

Felicia sighed, softening. "Then stop helping. Go marry your UFC Dick Print. Live off room service. Send me postcards from the Maldives titled 'Wish You Were Kneading.'"

I blew a rogue strand out of my face. Yesterday, I'd been lounging in a Vegas hotel robe, living my best *Real Housewives* meets *365 Days* fantasy. Today? Arguing over a café that felt less like a "passion project" and more like a *pyramid scheme* for baked goods.

Felicia, wielding a spatula like it was a courtroom gavel, wasn't finished. "Look, if you'd rather be shacked up with Eric than here, just say so! I'll Venmo you your 'investment' back in monthly installments of $5.99."

"With Eric?" I spluttered. "What's he got to do with my inability to tell margarine from butter?!"

She rolled her eyes, laugh-grunting. "Please. You've been half-assing this place since you started bumping uglies with him. We needed you Saturday! But nooo, you were too busy finding your long-lost vagina in a hotel minibar!"

I barked a laugh sharper than a shard of glass. "I practically took annual leave for this! I've baked so many tarts, I dream in pastry! I've worked the till, the grinder, the espresso machine from hell—and I'm here all the time, Fel. It's not fair."

Felicia snatched my dough—a sad, lumpy thing that resembled a stress ball—and frisbee'd it into the trash. "Face it, Eva. You're about as committed to this café as I am to veganism."

I gaped. "You think I went to the Cosmopolitan to *spite you*? It had nothing to do with you."

Well, it *does* have something to do with me!" Felicia barked. "If I hadn't suggested a staycation, you'd still be eyeing Eric across the café like a nervous raccoon hoarding croissants!"

The guilt I'd been stockpiling over Felicia's "I've-slept-in-the-kitchen-twice-this-week" martyrdom and her dating life drier than a gluten-free brownie cracked like over baked shortcrust. (See! I was learning!)

"Eric planned it! I just agreed!" I shot back, flinging a rogue raisin at her. "And for the record, raccoons are highly resourceful!"

The argument escalated faster than Level 1 emergency. Felicia accused me of abandoning our business in its moment of need while I countered that her idea of "teamwork" was just me being her unpaid dough lackey.

Deep down, I got it. Felicia had poured her soul into this café, and her idea of "sharing the dream" was basically assigning me the role of Comic Relief Sous Chef. But honestly, I'd rather have been waterboarded with matcha powder than admit she had a point.

Then she went nuclear. "You're only with Eric because I manifested it during that full moon tarot night!"

Oh, please. The only thing Felicia "manifested" that night was a parking ticket and a questionable decision to text her ex.

"I'm leaving," I announced, wrestling off my apron—now less "baker-chic" and more "floury crime scene." "Find another ride home. Maybe ask that sourdough starter you love so much."

"You're *fired*!" she shouted, as I stormed out, the door

slamming so hard it knocked a "World's Best Barista" mug off the shelf.

Outside, I half-expected a studio audience to pop out and rate our performance. *Solid 4/10. Needs more dramatic pastry throwing... and a few more erroneous name calling.*

*"Your postcoital glow must be *rage*, because *wow*, Eva—you're giving off major 'I'll cut you' vibes," Lexi drawled, swirling her strawberry lemonade like she was auditioning for *Real Housewives of Scrubs & Crocs*.

Claire snorted into her spaghetti. "Isn't sex supposed to make you... I don't know, less homicidal? Or at least *marginally* pleasant?"

I glared at my salad, regretting my life choices. *Why had I ordered rabbit food when the carbonara was calling my name like a siren?*

After my *Great Bake-Off Blowout* with Felicia, I'd thrown myself into work like a woman possessed. I'd even volunteered to tackle the e-filing—a task so soul-crushing, it made trash TV look like Shakespeare. But no amount of filing or medical records could drown out the frustration bubbling inside me like a poorly proofed sourdough.

"Drop it," I muttered, my cheeks flaming. If it weren't for Felicia's dough-tastrophe, I'd probably be glowing like a L'Oréal ad right now.

Even Eric's sweet "good morning" text—complete with a heart emoji and a "Miss you already"—hadn't lifted my mood. The man had been snoring while Felicia and I were one spatula away from a *Jerry Springer* showdown.

"It can't have been that bad," Claire said, tilting her head like a confused golden retriever. "Eric looks like he knows his way around a... bedroom."

I shot her a look that could curdle milk. *Oh, sure, Claire. Easy for you to say when your sex life's been on hiatus since the maternity ward.* But I wasn't about to go full villain on her.

"Who knew Eric Mann was a *dud* in bed?" Lexi smirked, earning a cackle from Claire.

I should've called in sick. Or faked my own death. Anything to avoid this. But going home wasn't an option either—not with Felicia's stuff scattered everywhere like breadcrumbs from a bad breakup.

"It's not Eric," I snapped, launching into the full saga of my café meltdown.

Claire sighed like she'd seen this coming since Series 1,

Episode 1.

"I knew it. I *knew* this would happen."

"How?"

She twirled her pasta with the precision of a true Italian (American Italian, because Claire knew zilch about her roots). "Eva, you can't *force* passion. Running a café isn't like binge-watching *Bake Off* thinking it's all fun and games—it's hard. Felicia meant well, but she wasn't thinking about *you*. She was thinking about her vision board and dragged you along for the ride."

I nodded, letting Claire's words sink in like a good moisturizer. "She just assumed I'd be grateful—like I'd won the lottery or something. But running a café isn't exactly my idea of a jackpot."

"Felicia's always been a bit… enthusiastic," Lexi said, swirling her fork like she was diagnosing a rare disease. "But I think she meant well. Deep down. Very deep down."

Claire gasped, her fork hovering mid-air. "Wait—you don't think this is about the café, do you? It's about Eric."

Bingo.

"I'm not saying she's jealous," Lexi clarified, stabbing a piece of pasta. "But let's be real—her last 'relationship' was with a guy who thought *Twilight* was a documentary.

Meanwhile, you've got Eric Mann—UFC hunk, human golden retriever, and apparently a pro at planning staycations. It's not exactly a fair comparison."

Claire nodded sagely. "She's lashing out because she's feeling left out. And let's face it—you're an easy target. You're basically the emotional equivalent of a stress ball."

I crossed my arms. "Well, maybe I'm done being squeezed."

Felicia had pulled a lot over the years. The time she "accidentally" dyed my favorite romper pink. The time she "forgot" to tell me about that one finale watch party. The time she—*never mind*. Point is, I always let it slide. But this? This felt different.

"You know," Lexi said, her tone shifting to new levels of seriousness, "you could just be an investor. Take your cut, step back, and let Felicia handle the baking disasters."

"We're already 50/50," I pointed out. "And I'm the one covering salaries when the till's looking sadder than a sad animal bait video."

Lexi raised an eyebrow. "And what about Guy? Isn't he bleeding you dry?"

I groaned. "Don't even get me started. Felicia's 'genius' deal with him means he gets his cut every month, no matter what. The café makes money, but not enough to cover him *and* the bills. It's like running a marathon with a backpack full of bricks."

"Sounds like Felicia needs a financial advisor," Claire muttered, polishing off her wine.

Lexi nodded, her expression shifting to *Shark Tank* levels of intensity. "So, let me get this straight. You bake, you man the till, you basically run around like a chicken on Red Bull—but you're not actually getting paid for it?"

I nodded. "Pretty much. I mean, I cover salaries when the café's profits can't. So, yeah, I'm pulling my weight. Just not in a Michelin-starred chef kind of way."

"Right," Lexi said, leaning back like she'd just cracked the Da Vinci Code. "So here's the plan. You become an investor. You throw in cash, take a cut of the profits, and let Felicia and Shane handle the day-to-day chaos. No more tart-induced stress. No more espresso machine meltdowns. Just a little bit of money to fix the problem."

"An investor…" I repeated, the idea sparking like a faulty toaster. "You really think Felicia would go for it?"

Claire snorted. "What's her alternative? Challenging you to a *Bake Off* duel? Because, no offense, Eva, but you'd lose. Badly."

Lexi smirked. "She doesn't have a choice. You're the one keeping the lights on. Literally."

The weight on my shoulders—which had been roughly the size of a UPS delivery van—suddenly felt a little lighter. Could it really be that simple? Could I finally step back, reclaim my weekends, and go back to being the customer who orders a cortado and *doesn't* cry into her tart?

"I guess I could talk to her," I said, hesitating. "Assuming she hasn't already blocked my number and cursed me with a lifetime of soggy bottoms."

"Enough about the café," Lexi said, leaning forward with the kind of grin usually reserved for a different type of gossip —*men*. "Spill. Everything."

She meant Eric, of course.

And as I started talking—about the champagne, the poolside giggles, the way he'd looked at me like I was the only person in Vegas—I realized something.

I *did* have that post-staycation glow.

And it wasn't just from the sun.

CHAPTER

THIRTEEN

THE FISH TACO BAR was heaving like a Black Friday sale at H&M—every booth crammed, every stool occupied, and the air thick with the scent of lime and mild panic. Yet, despite the chaos, Eric and I might as well have been royalty. Or, more accurately, *Eric* was royalty. I was just the vaguely floral-scented handbag hanging off his arm.

Lexi had warned me dating a UFC star came with perks, but she'd failed to mention the downside: becoming invisible to anyone holding a drinks menu. The bartender—a woman with hair so sleek I suspected she conditioned it with liquid titanium—lit up like a Christmas tree when Eric approached. "Mr. Mann!" she trilled, ignoring me so thoroughly I half-wondered if I'd accidentally mastered the art of camouflage.

"And two fish tacos and a rosé for this lovely lady, please," Eric said, nodding at me like I was a human accessory he'd acquired en route.

The bartender's eyes snapped to mine, as if I'd materialized out of thin air. "*Oh!* Of course! Rosé, you said? Lovely choice." Her tone suggested she'd have complimented me for ordering battery acid if it meant Eric's tip.

The tacos arrived faster than if A-Train had personally delivered them, piled high with guac and a side of excessive lime wedges. I took a bite, and—*holy hell*—they were divine. Crispy, zesty, *life-affirming*. Who needs San Diego when you've got this place? And in the valley, too. For a moment, I forgot I'd been overlooked. Just for a moment.

Scanning the room, I noticed a pattern: the bartender's "tip-seeking sonar" only pinged for men. Women had to wave like shipwreck survivors to get a napkin. "She's got a type," I muttered, gesturing at a guy in a Hawaiian shirt getting his fourth margarita, this one compliments of the house for waiting two seconds too long.

Eric grinned, swiping taco sauce off his chin with a grin. "Want another drink? I'll throw a flare this time."

I giggled, the rosé warming me like a true desert sunset. "If I have another, you'll need to wheelbarrow me to the car."

"Bartender!" Eric called, grinning like a man who'd just discovered the secret to eternal happiness. We clinked glasses, and I decided one more rosé wouldn't hurt—though I made a mental note to avoid my signature move: "tipsy Eva" morphing into "Eva, Destroyer of Dignity." Eric still hadn't spilled the beans about that night—the one where I'd done fun blackout things (allegedly)—but I'd decided ignorance was bliss. If "fun drunk" was the worst of it, I'd take it.

The drinks arrived faster than a cheetah on an espresso bender. By sunset, the bar was heaving, and the guy beside me spotted Eric, elbowing me aside like I was a Target cart in the cookie aisle. Eric handled the fan with the grace of a true pro, but his hand found my knee under the bar, squeezing gently. (Translation: "I'm right here. This guy'll leave soon enough.")

As the night wore on, fans flocked like seagulls. Eric posed for selfies, signed napkins, and nodded politely as a man breathlessly explained how he'd "almost" gone pro in MMA (spoiler: he hadn't). Meanwhile, I sipped my wine, marveling at how fame turned a casual taco night into a TMZ hunt.

Finally, Eric tossed cash on the bar—enough to fund a small yacht—and whisked me out, abandoning our half-finished drinks.

"Sorry," he said, buckling up. "It can be a bit too much

sometimes."

"You're basically Vegas royalty," I said, fumbling with my seatbelt. "But, the bigger question is: are you sober enough to drive?"

He shot me a look. "I had *one* beer. You had three rosés."

"Wine doesn't count," I scoffed. "It's basically fruit juice with a PhD."

"Tell that to my mom," he laughed, pulling onto the Strip.

"I want to meet her," I blurted, then clapped a hand over my mouth like I'd just confessed to stealing the Constitution. *Great, Eva. Nothing says "I'm a keeper" like demanding a meet-the-parents moment after three rosés.*

Eric chuckled, unfazed. "She wants to meet you too. Next time she's in town, promise."

I slumped against the car window, the glass cool on my cheek as his words wrapped around me like a cashmere hug. This thing with Eric wasn't just real—it was *rom-com montage* real. Next stop: our moms bonding over tea and passive-aggressive recipes, plotting our wedding while we awkwardly smiled through it.

At the next red light, he laced his fingers through mine, leaning in for a kiss that tasted like mint chocolate.

"Can I ask what happened with Felicia?" Eric said suddenly, pulling back just as the light turned green.

"What happened with what?" I stalled.

"Claire called. Said you two had a fight about the café."

"Claire called you?!" I squawked. So much for sisterhood—Claire was out here playing couples' therapist with my drama. "It's nothing. Felicia's just… being Felicia. Thinks I should run the café like some Martha Stewart protégé, even though I can't tell a croissant from a crisis."

Eric's brow furrowed. "Why's she pushing you?"

"Because she's delusional!" I threw my hands up, nearly swatting the rearview mirror. "I'm a consumer, Eric. I buy coffee, I don't *make* it. The closest I've come to 'business strategy' is choosing oat milk over almond."

He grinned. "You do love that Saturday cortado…"

"Drinking it, not *crafting* it! I'm more likely to flood the place with espresso shots than turn a profit."

"I liked running into you there," he said softly, his thumb brushing my knuckle. "All sweaty in your leggings, glaring at the menu with that cute little squint."

"Sweaty?" I gasped. "I prefer 'glistening.' And you in those see-through sweats. *Distracting.*"

"See-through?" He laughed a nervous laugh. "Are we talking 'subtle print' or 'X-rated linen'?"

"Full see-through. You can see everything. And I do mean *everything*."

He ran a worried hand across his chin. "You don't say."

"And Felicia would say—"

"Okay," he cut in, clapping a hand over my mouth like he was silencing a rogue kazoo. "We've established my gym sweats are a public service. Moving on."

We dissolved into giggles, the stress of the day evaporating faster than champagne bubbles. "And now you're taking me home after our nice little date," I teased, batting my eyelashes.

"And now I'm taking you home after a nice little date," he echoed, pulling up to my apartment with a grin. His hand lingered on my knee. "Wish you'd come back to mine. My bed's tragically empty right now and wistfully inviting."

"Can't," I groaned, though every fibre of my rosé-soaked brain screamed "Yes!" "I've got a 5 a.m. date with a sourdough starter. It's *very* jealous."

He slumped like a kicked puppy. "So this sourdough's my rival now? Should I challenge it to a cage match?"

"Yes. Loser buys croissants." A thought struck me—bold,

buzzed, *brilliant*. "Speaking of... could your UFC buddies do a meet-and-greet at the café? *Please?* We're one stale muffin away from collapse."

Eric didn't blink. "Done. I'll drag the whole squad. We'll flex by the espresso machine. Call it... Caffeine & Cage Fights."

I kissed him, hard. "You're a *genius*. And not just because of the sweats."

He leaned in, breath warm against my ear. "Miss you in my bed, Eva."

Temptation wrapped in biceps. But I'd already hit snooze on my alarm twice this week.

"Gotta bake, babe. Priorities."

"I see," he groaned. "This is a problem, then."

"I keep telling you. Goodnight, Eric," I said, wrenching myself free.

As he drove off, a pang of regret filled me. *Sigh*. But at least I'd get to tell Felicia, "Surprise! Your café's hosting a muscle buffet."

"So, Eric's agreed to a meet-and-greet," I announced to Felicia, breezing into the kitchen like I hadn't been avoiding her for days. The air between us was frostier than a Costco freezer aisle, but hey—we shared a Wi-Fi password. We were practically married.

"Cool," Felicia muttered, eyes glued to her phone.

"Details pending," I added, retreating toward my room. "But prepare for an influx of biceps. And possibly protein powder."

I'd just shimmied one leg into pajama shorts printed with "Napping Champion 2023" when Felicia stormed in, wielding a half-eaten granola bar. "I'm *not* jealous of you," she declared. "Or your relationship."

I froze, mid-shimmy. "I know. I mean, unless you're after Eric's gym playlist. It's just aggressive grunting."

"Everyone thinks I'm jealous, but I'm not. I'm *happy* for you," she insisted, flopping onto my bed. "But the café... I thought adding you to the deed would be like, 'Yay, business besties!' Not... whatever it's turned out to be."

"Felicia, I can't even keep a houseplant alive. You handed me a *café*. I'm out of my depth."

She snorted, then sighed. "I just wanted to share it with you. But maybe I... overshot."

Before I could reply, she lunged at me. I braced for a slap but instead, she hugged me. A real, full-on hug.

"I'm sorry," she mumbled into my shoulder. "I turned you into a reluctant bakery warlord."

I patted her back, my anger dissolving faster than sugar in a latte. "It's okay. We'll fix it. Or sell it to Starbucks. Their cake pops don't cry during kneading."

"I've made a mess of it all, haven't I?" Felicia wailed, her grip around me tightening like a malfunctioning seatbelt. Her curls—a chaotic halo of coconut-scented springs—tickled my nose.

I patted her back, dodging a rogue curl. "It's fine! We've survived worse. Remember that apartment with the 'vintage charm'—aka the moldy shower curtain? We nailed that."

She pulled back, sniffling dramatically. "But I wanted this to be perfect."

"And it will be!" I chirped, swiping a tear off her cheek with my thumb. "Just wait till you hear Lexi's idea. It's genius. Like, *Shark Tank* meets *2 Broke Girls* genius."

Felicia blinked, mascara smudged. "What idea?"

"Patience, grasshopper."

She blew her nose into a crumpled receipt, then twisted her hair into a bun so aggressively, I feared for her scalp. But there it was—the Felicia I knew. Crisis averted, replaced by the steely resolve of a woman who once haggled a $200 sofa down to $50.

"So," she said, flopping onto my bed, "how *was* it?"

I hugged a pillow, grinning. "Nice. Really nice. You know Eric's, like, recognizably famous? People asked for selfies. One guy even asked him to sign a napkin. A *napkin*, Felicia. Who does that?"

She rolled her eyes, smiling. "Uh, *everyone*? His last fight trended on TikTok. My dentist follows him."

"Yes, but it's different seeing it in real life, as in, outside the café."

She threw a pillow at my head. "Not the UFC gossip, you walnut! The *staycation*. Spill. Now."

"Oh! *That.*" I flopped back, star-fishing beside her. "Okay, so first, there was champagne. Then, Dick Print sweats—"

We talked until 2 a.m., dissecting every detail—the tacos, the kisses, the way Eric's biceps flexed when he opened the mini-bar. Felicia eventually conked out mid-sentence, snoring into my purple pillowcase. I draped a blanket over her, whispering, "Night, Candace Nelson."

The next morning, her alarm blared Dua Lipa at a

decibel usually reserved for nuclear warnings. We stumbled to the café, fueled by espresso shots and questionable decisions, ready to tackle another baking lesson. Or, as Felicia called it, "Sourdough Wars: The Reckoning."

CHAPTER

FOURTEEN

GIRLS' NIGHT HAD BECOME as rare as a decent Wi-Fi signal in our café's storage room—which, for the record, was also home to a family of mice who'd developed a worrying addiction to almond croissant crumbs. Between Felicia's baking marathons and my newfound hobby of "dating a man who thinks burpees are foreplay," we were both running on fumes. Felicia kept muttering about "cutting costs," and I lived in mortal fear she'd unplug the AC to save $50 a week, leaving us with an oven-created heat that would rival the coming summer temperatures.

The rest of the girls were off scheming like characters in a Jane Austen novel—if Jane Austen wrote about gold diggers and UFC fighters. Lexi had upgraded from flirting with bankers to full-time romancing Charles, a man whose idea of "fixing things" involved throwing money at problems

(Lexi) until they sparkled. Meanwhile, Claire—bless her meddling heart—had been playing Mystery Mediator between me and Felicia, which explained why Eric kept texting things like, "Claire says you like peonies???" with no context.

But tonight, *finally*, we'd carved out time for girls' night. I arrived early at Cali's, as usual, eager to inhale the scent of something other than espresso beans and regret. Rubi, now a tiny tornado in polka-dot leggings, sprinted past me with a crayon clutched in her fist. I scooped her up, blowing raspberries on her belly while she giggled like a drunk pixie. "Tia Eva's here to corrupt you with sugar!" I whispered. Cali shot me a look. "She's already had three cookies. Don't you dare."

As I unloaded my drama—Felicia's baking tyranny, Eric's baffling bicep-themed pick-up lines—Cali rubbed her watermelon-sized bump and sighed. "This one's due November 3rd, but he's tap-dancing on my bladder like he's aiming for a Halloween debut." She groaned. "A Halloween baby? How am I supposed to host a spooky soiree *and* a birthday party every year?"

I gasped. "Dual-themed parties! Witches *and* cake! Ghosts *and* piñatas! It's genius!"

"Or a nightmare," Cali muttered, waddling to the fridge

for pickles and ice cream. "Imagine coordinating costumes and goodie bags while sleep-deprived. I'll look like a zombie bride forever."

"You'll be fabulous," I insisted, stealing a pickle. "And if not, we'll just blame the kids. Parenting hack."

Cali was pacing her living room like a caffeinated flamingo filled with useless worry. "What if he comes early? What if he likes spiders? What if—"

"Wine," I declared, thrusting a bottle of Pinot Gris toward her like a magic wand. "One sip can't harm, right? I think I read that somewhere."

She gave me a look. "Absolutely not. I'd rather mainline kale smoothies."

"Suit yourself," I shrugged, pouring myself a generous glass. "But if this baby arrives on Halloween, you're naming him Casper. No take-backs."

When I launched into the Felicia saga, Cali—ever the diplomat—nodded along until I mentioned the café deed. "Felicia's a saint for adding you," she insisted, nibbling a celery stick with judgy precision. "You should be grateful. Not everyone gets handed a business like a Chipotle loyalty card."

"I didn't want a business!" I protested. "I wanted a

cortado and a quiet corner to read. Now I'm trapped in a *Great British Bake Off* nightmare, except Paul Hollywood's replaced by Felicia and her baking sermons."

Cali softened, crunching thoughtfully. "Okay, fair. But you're acting like Felicia's a villain twirling a croissant mustache. She's just enthusiastic."

"Enthusiastic?" I snorted. "She's like a Mafia don in a 'Live, Laugh, Bake' apron. First Lexi, now me—next she'll strong-arm Rubi into kneading dough."

"Eva," Cali sighed, rubbing her bump like a crystal ball, "if people let Felicia boss them around, that's their problem. You agreed to the deed. *You* signed the papers. *You—*"

"—am a spineless jellyfish," I finished, slumping onto her sofa. "I know."

A pause. Then, quieter: "Would you have added her? If it were your café?"

I froze, celery mid-air. "I… Well. *Hm.*"

"Exactly."

Felicia's intentions were probably purer than organic flour, but the question lingered like a stale muffin scent. Had I been gifted a golden ticket—or quietly enrolled in a cult of caffeine and money pits?

"Look," Cali said, tossing a doll into Rubi's toy bin,

"Felicia loves you. Even if her love language is a little aggressive baking session."

I sipped my wine, eyeing Rubi's crayon mural on the wall. Maybe Cali was right. Maybe Felicia wasn't a villain. Just a zealot in a flour-dusted apron, trying to drag me into her carb-loaded utopia.

The girls arrived like a flock one right after the other, all chatter and clinking jewelry, as Jason—Cali's eternally patient husband—scooped up Rubi and retreated inside, muttering something about football. Cali whipped up a batch of spicy margaritas so potent they could've doubled as hand sanitizer. When I praised her skills, she stared longingly at my glass, sighing like a kid barred from a candy store. "One sip," I whispered conspiratorially. She swatted my hand away. "Stop it, Eva."

Wrapped in a blanket, I sipped my frosty drink while Lexi launched into her latest Charles update. "He's literally rewriting his will for me," she announced, flipping her hair. "And he booked us a private island. And he's firing his interior designer because I hate taupe."

Felicia snorted. "Let me guess—the island comes with a prenup-shaped bow?"

Lexi's eyes narrowed, stormy gray turning thunderous. "Charles is winning me back. There's no prenup, just *dolla' bills*."

"Expensive," Claire added, crunching an ice cube.

Felicia added, "So, it won't be Charles who gets you back —it'll be his money."

I jumped in before Lexi could retort, and gave her a pointed look. "What about Scott? Any chance he'll slither back from Phuket?"

Lexi smirked. "Funny you ask, because Charles is persuading him to face the music. Though 'persuading' might involve a yacht, a subpoena, and a very surprised Tegan." She sipped her drink, smug she was this close to pulling it off. "Love makes men creative, babe."

Claire leaned in, eyes wide. "But will you marry Charles, or just take his money and dip?"

"Undecided. Ages ago, all I wanted was a no-prenup wedding, but now I want more. No prenup *and* Scott's offshore millions," Lexi declared, tossing her hair. The girls gasped in unison—a sound Lexi clearly loved.

"How?" Felicia blurted, her face scrunching. "You're going to erotic asphyxiate your way into his life too? Or is Charles just your middleman in this international crime spree?"

Lexi recoiled. "Erotic asphyxiation? Felicia, that's what

Tinder swipes are for. I'm a luxury gold digger, not a serial killer."

I waved my margarita, cutting the tension. "Charles is doing the heavy lifting. Lexi's just art directing."

"Exactly," Lexi purred, sipping her drink with grace and charm. "Scott's got a Norwegian passport under 'Bjørn McHotstuff' and a private jet on standby. All he needs is a brown combover, some Botox for that schnoz—"

"Rudolph called," I interjected. "He wants his nose back."

Lexi cackled. "Charles is already on it. Next stop: *Mission Impossible*."

Felicia rolled her eyes, not enjoying Lexi's storytelling. "Fake passports only work in *Jason Bourne* movies, Lexi. Real life has extradition treaties and Homeland Security."

"For peasants, maybe," Lexi sniffed. "Scott has his way of bribing officers or whoever. It's ethical corruption."

Claire chimed in, "And he's got all that stolen cash! He could buy a country. Or at least a really nice yacht."

Cali, rubbing her bump, leaned forward. "But how do *you* end up with the money, Lex? Charles isn't just handing it over, is he?"

Lexi's grin turned Cheshire. "Babe, Charles will funnel it

through shell companies named things like 'Luxe Love LLC.' A little here, a little there—enough for a chateau, not enough for Interpol to care." She paused, swirling her drink. "Romance isn't dead. It's just *offshore*."

Felicia couldn't drop it. "So you're *not* a criminal mastermind, just a *romantic consultant* to one? Groundbreaking."

Lexi leaned back, sipping her margarita like it was a trophy. "Sweetie, if Charles can't launder money *and* his reputation, he doesn't deserve this." She fluttered her lashes at an imaginary paparazzo. "Besides, hitching is *optional*. Hitching is flexible. Money isn't."

"Poor Charles," I piped in. "All he wanted was a gold digger, not a Nobel Prize in tax evasion and a chance at Guantanamo." The girls cackled, and I basked in my two seconds of stand-up glory.

Felicia, ever the buzzkill, pivoted like a lawyer mid-cross-examination. "Why isn't Tegan here? Did she finally realize you're all lunatics?"

"Tegan," I snapped, "is not part of our support group. Keep up."

Claire—bless her meddling soul—chimed in, crunching ice like it was courtroom evidence. "And didn't Tegan ban Eric talk? Eva's been muttering about it for weeks. Very

Mean Girls of her."

Cali gasped, clutching her bump. "She banned Eric? How do you mean?"

I groaned. "It wasn't just Tegan. These two—" I jabbed a lime wedge at Lexi and Felicia, "—acted like mentioning Eric's name would summon a demon. Or worse, Tegan's divorce lawyer."

"It was a sensitive time!" Lexi and Felicia chorused, their unity almost touching. If by "touching" you mean "mildly terrifying."

"I don't care if Tegan's sensitive," I said, borrowing Felicia's courtroom glare. "My love life isn't a classified document to be opened *only* when Tegan's not around. And *Claire*—" I turned on her, "—why'd you snitch to Eric about my fight with Felicia? Are you running a gossip hotline now?"

Claire's eyes widened, her "Who, me?" face so polished it could've been trademarked. "He *told* you? He promised he wouldn't!"

"Of course he did," I deadpanned. "Next time, meddle louder. Maybe hire a skywriter: 'Eva's Pissed. Send help.'"

Felicia snorted into her drink. "I'd chip in for that."

The conversation swerved toward me like a shopping cart

with a wonky wheel, the girls piling on with the subtlety of a *Survivor* voting round. "Imagine if I called Marc to whine about your pissy attitude at work!" Claire only gasped. The group solemnly agreed that while Felicia and I would've eventually hugged it out between passive-aggressive Post-it notes, Claire's meddling deserved a "Well-Meaning But Nosy" trophy.

Then came the interrogation: "Are Eric's thrusts as powerful as his biceps?" Lexi purred. "Does he close his eyes to keep them open?"

"Lexi!"

"He was lovely over the phone," Claire sighed, batting her lashes like Eric had personally cured world hunger. "Said he'd talk to Eva but 'couldn't promise anything'—very Mr. Darcy of him."

"And you," Lexi jabbed her straw at me, "were obsessed with 'ending your celibacy.' You talked about it more than I do about Botox!"

"Lies!" I squawked. "I was focused on emotional intimacy! The connection! Had nothing to do with Tegan's nasty—"

"The connection?" Felicia snorted. "Eva, you described his Dick Print as—.'"

"Felicia!"

The debate devolved into chaos—Felicia insisting I'd doodled "Mrs. Eva Mann" on café napkins, Lexi swearing I'd once called his abs "the Eighth Wonder of the World." Claire, ever the devil's advocate, mused, "But how was it?"

I straightened up, blanket clutched like a royal cape. "Oh. My. God. Buckle up, ladies."

Cue the giggles, the gasps, the "No she didn't!" shrieks as I spilled every PG-13 detail of the Cosmopolitan night—the champagne, the see-through sweats, the way Eric had somehow made "Do you prefer firm or soft pillows?" sound like a marriage proposal. We laughed until our cheeks hurt, Lexi demanding a reenactment ("Show us the smolder!"), Felicia grudgingly admitting Eric had "potential," and Cali texting Jason: "Bring more tequila. And earplugs."

By midnight, we were a pile of empty glasses and half-eaten guac, the fight with Felicia forgotten—or at least buried under a mountain of margarita-fueled gossip. Because that's the thing about friends: they're equal parts therapists, comedians, and *extremely* nosy biographers.

CHAPTER

FIFTEEN

❧

HALLOWEEN LOOMED LIKE A glitter-covered guillotine, and as a newly minted member of the Couples' Costume Industrial Complex, I was drowning in panic. Eric had casually dropped, "We should dress up!" as if suggesting a coffee date, not a high-stakes cosplay referendum. Two weeks?! I hadn't planned a costume since the Great "Sexy Pizza Slice" Debacle of 2018 (never again). Now I faced a Spirit Halloween pop-up that resembled a post-apocalyptic craft store, staffed by teenagers who definitely thought "Mr. Darcy" was a TikTok influencer.

The racks offered horrors worse than any haunted house: a "Cop & Robber" set where the handcuffs looked suspiciously like leftover IKEA drawer pulls, a "Caveman Duo" featuring a loincloth thinner than my patience, and a "Zombie Doctor" costume that screamed "I gave up on life *and* Halloween." I craved originality—*Bridgerton* meets *Rocky*, or Shrek and Fiona if Eric embraced green body paint. But no. We'd likely end up as "Generic UFC Guy & Woman Who Forgot to Try," courtesy of a store that would vanish November 1st, leaving only a trail of polyester and regret.

My fatal error had been bringing Cali along, 8 and a half months pregnant and radiating the chaotic energy of a squirrel on espresso, she drifted through aisles like a zombie bride, muttering about "family themes" and "expandable costumes." "What if the baby comes early? Do I buy a three-person astronaut set or a four-person Jurassic Park? What if he hates dinosaurs?"

"Cali," I said, holding up a baby Yoda onesie, "this fits anyone from newborn to nihilist teen. Just… grab it."

"But Jason wants us to be *Star Wars*," she sighed, as if her husband—a man who once wore mismatched socks to a wedding—was the Coachella of themed parenting. "What if the baby arrives Halloween night? Do I dare go into labor in Chewbacca fur?!"

"You absolutely can't," I agreed, nodding solemnly, as if questioning Cali's costume logic might trigger a hormonal apocalypse. One wrong move and we'd both be buried under a Pyramid of Maternity Jeans.

Cali hovered over a clown costume, her face twisted in existential despair. "Maybe I should just… commit to the clown life. Jason can be a juggler. Rubi's a tiny unicyclist. The baby? A balloon animal."

"Or," I said, steering her toward a family of fuzzy bear costumes, "we could avoid traumatizing your newborn with creepy circus-core." The bear set was adorable—if you ignored the fact that the baby bear size was mysteriously missing, leaving the cub-shaped hole in Cali's heart wider than a Black Friday check-out line.

"It's almost perfect," she sighed, clutching the bear ears with more force than Eric's bicep curl. "But without the baby size, it's just incomplete. Like we're the Dysfunctional Bear Family who forgot a child at Walmart."

"*Target*," I declared, snapping my fingers like a suburban Sherlock. "We'll grab a newborn onesie with a bear face. If the baby arrives early, he'll fit in. If not, it'll just be a bear onesie. Win-win."

Cali's eyes welled up—a hormonal tsunami. "That's genius," she sniffed, as if I'd just invented fire.

Meanwhile, my own costume crisis raged on. Eric, bless his obliviousness, had texted: "Whatever u pick is cool :)". A green flag? Sure. But also code for: "I will wear head-to-toe spandex if it means I don't have to think."

As Cali triumphantly checked out with bear costumes for the win, I mentally scrolled through couples' ideas: Ken and Barbie (too basic), Bonnie and Clyde (too felonious), Shrek and Fiona (...tempting). But nothing screamed "We're a UFC power couple."

On the drive to Chik-Fil-A for a nice lunch break, my mind drifted to Felicia. After weeks of café-induced panic attacks, I'd decided to bail on Biz Eva and reclaim Chill Eva. Lexi, our resident *Wolf of Wall Street* (if the Wolf wore Louboutins and bribed sugar daddies), had schooled me on becoming a "silent investor"—a fancy term for "pay the bills and flee." All I needed was to catch Felicia in a rare moment of joy—perhaps mid-sip of a pumpkin spice latte—before dropping the news. "Congrats! You're free to micromanage alone!"

Cali popped a chicken nugget into her mouth. "Finally," she sighed, crumbs tumbling onto her bump. "A nugget in the wilderness. I was starting to think we'd have to survive on kale smoothies and hope."

"You live in the suburbs, Cal," I said, stealing a waffle fry. "The only 'wilderness' here is the PTA WhatsApp group."

She waved a nugget dismissively. "Don't ruin this for me. This sauce is my emotional support animal now."

My phone buzzed—Felicia. I answered, mouth full. "Hey,

what's—"

"Are you near?" Felicia's voice was a panicked screech. "I've had an accident."

I choked, fry lodged in my throat. "Accident?! Are you—are you bleeding?!"

Cali froze, mid-dip. "Bleeding?!" she mouthed, clutching her bump like it might flee.

"The La Marzocco!" Felicia wailed. "I broke the espresso machine. It's… gushing steam. Like a tea kettle possessed by Satan."

I slumped against the booth, deflating. "Oh, that kind of accident. For a second, I thought you'd recreated *The Hangover* in the café."

"Eva, this is serious! We can't function with one machine. It's peak pumpkin spice season!"

"Right, right. National emergency." I eyed Cali, now stress-eating nuggets like they held answers. "I'll hit Target. But Felicia, the replacement will be a *Target* machine. It won't have 'artisanal soul' or whatever you call it."

"Just hurry," she hissed, as if I'd suggested serving instant coffee.

At Target, Cali waddled beside me like a penguin in maternity leggings, pausing to marvel at Halloween candy.

"Could Rubi be a Skittles piñata? Too on-the-nose?"

"Focus," I said, dragging her to Appliances. The espresso machines sat smugly on the shelf, their boxes screaming "I make brown water, not crafted experiences!"

Cali pointed to the cheapest model, which resembled a 1990s fax machine. "This one's cute! Looks like Wall-E's cousin."

"Felicia would rather drink motor oil," I muttered, grabbing the mid-tier option—a steal at $499. "Then I'll have to make a return trip, and baby, I am done for the day."

Once out, I stared at the espresso machine box in my trunk, its cheerful logo taunting me like a neon reminder of my impending financial doom. Felicia would take one look at this shiny, soulless contraption and demand I return it for something with "artisan pedigree"—preferably gold-plated and blessed by a Venetian barista. But hey, at least my credit card was earning air miles! If I kept this up, maybe I'd finally afford that flight to Belize... or a coffin.

Cali leaned against my car, crunching a rogue waffle fry she'd smuggled from Chick-fil-A. "Felicia's gonna bankrupt you," she said, eyes wide with a mix of awe and horror. "Next thing you know, she'll ask you to fund a second location."

"No way," I groaned. "Last week it was 'when will we

make a profit?'"

After dropping Cali off—with strict instructions to text me if Baby "Name Pending" so much as sneezed—I faced the espresso machine again. The box loomed like a sarcastic brick. "Pilates arms," I muttered, channeling the ghost of every overpriced workout class I'd ever taken. Spoiler: they were useless. If Lexi were here, she'd have hired a shirtless moving crew billed to Charles' Amex. But no, I was Eva "Ethical Guilt" Torres, hauling appliances like a peasant.

Defeated, I teetered toward Eric's gym, a temple of grunts and protein farts. The smell hit me first—a cocktail of sweat, ambition, and Axe Body Spray. Inside, men bench-pressed small cars while women lunged in neon leggings, their ponytails whipping like battle flags.

Maybe it was love—or maybe I'd just gone nose-blind—but Eric didn't reek of the gym's usual cocktail of stale protein shakes and desperation. No, he smelled like… well, *him*. Comforting, *clean*. I barely flinched as I scanned the room, though my pulse did that traitorous little skip. His car was parked outside, so he *had* to be here. Funny, for a guy who looked like he'd been carved out of marble, he somehow blended into the chaos of grunting meatheads and clanging weights seamlessly. The gym had blown up after that viral video last spring—same as the café. And when Eric and Mindy started winning fights, suddenly everyone wanted a piece of this place. He didn't even own it, but I called it "his gym" anyway. Poetic license.

Brody spotted me before I could duck behind a rack of dumbbells. "Hey, Eva. Looking for Eric?"

Shirtless, dripping sweat, and grinning like a Labrador who'd just found a steak. *Now I get why Lexi keeps him around.* Charles, with his trust fund charm, couldn't compete —not in this arena. But Brody's temper was as legendary as his abs, so I kept my tone breezy. "Yeah. Need a hand outside."

"Eric!" he bellowed, loud enough to startle a guy mid-bench-press.

There he was, jumping rope like some fitness influencer's wet dream—shirt soaked, breathing ragged, all rhythmic thwacks and coiled muscle. "God help me," I muttered. At this point, I didn't care if we were both juggling flaming chainsaws. Tonight, I'd be climbing that man like a jungle gym.

"Eva," he said, jogging over, kissing me like we weren't in public, sweat transferring onto my cheek. I didn't wipe it off.

"Sorry to drag you away," I lied.

"Never a drag," he said, swiping a towel over his face.

"Just outside," I said, nodding toward the door. He

yanked on a sweatshirt—probably to avoid hypothermia, though part of me mourned the loss of the view—and hoisted the espresso machine box like it was filled with feathers.

Felicia gushed her thanks to *him*, not me, for "saving the day," ranting about how the café was one broken machine away from anarchy. My eye twitched. *I* sourced the damn thing. *I* negotiated the delivery. But now wasn't the time. I'd save that grenade for the "I quit" conversation brewing in my back pocket.

"Thanks," I said, still warm from the gym's ambiance. Then I did a double take. "You changed your sweats?"

He grinned. "The see-through ones? Yeah, that was kinda embarrassing."

"Wear them tonight," I said, smirking. "Pick me up at eight."

He laughed, tugging me into a hug that smelled like salt and effort, kissing my temple. "Babe, for you? I'll show up in a Speedo."

Woke up in Eric's bed—again. His room looked like a grayscale Instagram filter had thrown up on it. Even the damn alarm clock was gray. The only splash of color were those see-through sweats slung over the chair, a trophy from last night's *negotiations*. I smirked, remembering just when I'd slid them off him, stretching like a cat in a sunbeam, only to catch Eric watching me with that grin. You know the one —half smug, half "I've won the lottery and it's you."

"Morning, Snorezilla," he said, voice gravelly.

I snorted. "Please. You were the one serenading me with a fart symphony. *Bravo*, maestro."

A blush crept up his neck—adorable on a guy built like a Viking—before he yanked the duvet over our heads. "One more sound and I'll recreate the encore," he threatened, all fake menace. "Unless you shut me up properly."

So I did. Thoroughly. His mouth was warm and slow, all Sunday-morning laziness and last-night's promises.

"Now," he murmured, hands roaming, "about those costumes…"

Right. The Halloween thing we'd *sworn* we'd plan today. But his thumb was tracing my hipbone, and suddenly, coordinating couple's outfits felt as urgent as folding laundry.

"Later," I said, tangling my legs with his.

He laughed, low and wicked. "Fine by me."

CHAPTER

SIXTEEN

THE CAFÉ WAS THROBBING like a nightclub at 2 a.m.—even though we'd closed hours ago. Felicia waltzed in late, but honestly, after the week we'd had? I'd have forgiven her for showing up in a snorkel and flippers. Running this place was like herding feral cats, and that was before you factored in dead weight. *Cough*—yours truly—*cough*.

Somehow, the four of us—Felicia, Shane, Lexi, and the World's Most Reluctant Barista (hi)—had slapped this place into shape in half a day. Eric and his UFC crew were too busy grunting at weights to lift a finger, which was fine. *Totally fine*. The man was laser-focused on his next fight, and right now, his idea of foreplay was protein shakes and sparring tapes.

But credit where it's due: Lexi's years of drilling me in "gold digger chic" paid off. The café looked like Tim Burton and Martha Stewart had a Halloween baby. Fog machines? Check. Motion-activated ghouls that made grown men yelp? Check. Lexi's original pitch involved aerialists swinging from the rafters, but Felicia and I vetoed that faster than you can say "liability waiver." Eric's wallet was already funding this spooktacular, and the last thing I needed was him footing the bill for Cirque du Soleil's hospital bills.

Speaking of Eric throwing cash around—he'd insisted on bankrolling the whole thing, worried our "little café" might get overshadowed by the valley's other haunted attractions. Pride stung, but his puppy-dog eyes won. Lexi called it a "strategic alliance." I called it… well, let's just say the man's generosity had perks. He'd handed over his Amex without a request for a tally, so that was that.

"Look at you!" Lexi crowed, spinning me in my JLo-wannabe dress—a shockingly good Nordstrom Rack find. "Little Eva, all grown up and *not* dressed like a haunted librarian!"

I flushed. "Shut up! You look great!"

Lexi had gone full Anna Nicole Smith—if Anna Nicole had raided a bridal boutique after three espresso martinis. Her platinum wig was defying gravity (and logic), her wedding dress was literally held together with safety pins, and she'd accessorized with a tiara that screamed "divorced by

Thursday." Charles, meanwhile, was slumped in a wheelchair playing her "elderly billionaire husband," which was either method acting or just his natural vibe. Honestly, the man looked like an assisted living resident who'd forgotten his cat.

I'd been hunting for Brody, who'd gone full Joker—purple suit, maniacal grin, weirdly on-brand—when I spotted him at the UFC table. Brody was busy taking selfies with fans, which was baffling because last I checked, his claim to fame was once spraining his ankle on a *Love Island* audition gone wrong. But hey, if it kept him from reigniting his on-again-off-again feud with Lexi, I'd let him cosplay as a celebrity. Turns out, half the crowd thought he was *actually* Jared Leto. Go figure.

"Eric funded the whole thing," I whispered to Lexi, gesturing at the fog machine belching smoke like a haunted steam engine. "Lights, props, even the $200 zombie that vomits glitter."

She arched a penciled brow. "And he's not charging you rent for his presence, right?"

"He refused payment. But the other fighters…?"

"Pfft. Let them keep the meet-and-greet cash," she said, waving a dismissive hand. "They're about as famous as my third cousin's pottery Instagram."

Across the room, Charles had parked his wheelchair by

the register like a disgruntled parking attendant, barking orders and hoarding lemon tarts. Every time a UFC fan wandered near, he'd yell, "This isn't a zoo!" I started to wonder if I'd hallucinated the whole Brody-Charles-Lexi love triangle. Maybe Charles was just… grouchy. A crotchety old gremlin who hated fun and loved pastries.

"He's taking this shockingly well," I muttered.

Lexi clapped a hand over my mouth. "*Shh!* The old fart's been sulking all day. Hates Brody's guts, but I told him—water under the bridge, darling! As long as he funds my shoe habit and signs over Scott's funds, I'll walk down the aisle. For real this time."

I glanced at Charles, now demanding a "low-fat oat milk latte" in a tone that suggested he'd never heard of joy. "He's really committing to the bit, huh?"

"Oh, he'll commit," Lexi purred, adjusting her tiara. "Or I'll upgrade to a newer model. Maybe a tech bro. Or a literal prince. He knows the drill."

We quietly giggled at that, but then she was storming off like Cinderella after curfew—because Charles dared to eat a tart without her. The tart in question was Felicia's masterpiece: cherry filling oozing out of pastry "severed fingers" so realistic, I half-expected them to crawl off the plate. Honestly, the thing belonged in a horror movie, or maybe a *very* niche baking competition. And thank God, because these tarts were selling faster than free Wi-Fi.

The crowd was bonkers. UFC fans, Halloween enthusiasts, and tart connoisseurs packed the place like we were giving away gold bars. I mean, if this many people would line up for a photo with Eric's biceps and a pastry shaped like a crime scene, maybe we *could* turn this café into a real business.

"Tegan's Instagram post basically broke the internet, right?" Felicia said, adjusting her Cardi B "Money" headdress, which had started sagging. She'd spent the week stress-baking and muttering about "supply chain issues" (translation: Shane ate all the chocolate sprinkles), but now she looked like a queen surveying her kingdom. A kingdom where Shane, dressed as Winnie the Pooh—or rather, in a Winnie the Pooh crop top—was manning the register with the panicked grin of someone who'd never counted change sober.

The door chimed, and in waddled Cali, her belly leading the charge like a GPS set to "waddle." Jason trailed behind, juggling baby Rubi, who was swaddled in a bear costume so fluffy, she resembled a sentient teddy. Jason beelined for the UFC table, grinning like he'd just spotted a cavity (or, you know, a UFC champion).

"I'm basically a human beach ball now," Cali said, looking around. "But *wow*. This place looks like a Tim Burton Pinterest board. I'm equal parts impressed and terrified."

"Mission accomplished," I said, eyeing a teenager who'd just yelped after biting into a "finger" tart.

I yanked Cali backward like she'd wandered into a lion enclosure when she neared a prop set to "nuclear screech." "Nope, not there. That mummy's cursed, and I refuse to deliver your baby in a room that smells of pumpkin spice and regret."

She wheezed a laugh, clutching her belly like it might detach. "I need to sit before I invent a new yoga pose: the suffocated whale."

"Let me tell Jason to skip the line," I announced, already power-walking toward Eric, who was posing with a UFC superfan sporting blue hair and a death grip on his bicep. "That's Jason—Cali's husband, *not* an actual bear—and Rubi's the tiny Ewok in his arms. Family discount!"

Eric, bless him, sprang into action like a superhero whose power is awkward small talk. He whisked Jason out of the line, bonding over... whatever men bond over. ("Bro, your dad-stache is iconic.") He even dashed to Cali, apologized for "diplomatic duties" (i.e.: flexing for photos), and promised brunch. Cali shot me a look that screamed, "Keep him."

For at least an hour, I floated around the café in a customer-service haze, refilling coffees and dodging toddlers hyped on sugar. Then Claire arrived with her *Grease* reboot: Sandy, Danny, and baby Kenickie, whose hair was slicked back with enough gel to waterproof a boat.

"*Stop it*," I cooed at baby Ethan, whose leather jacket was the size of a napkin. "You're the tiniest greaser in history. Do you even know what a carburetor is?"

Claire adjusted her Sandy curls, nervous. "The costumes took weeks. I had to bribe Marc with a PS5 to wear those pants."

"You look like you stepped out of a musical *and* a time machine," I said. And she did—Marc was rocking that white jacket like he'd stolen it from Travolta's closet.

As the guys huddled around Eric—bonding over UFC stats and dad jokes—Claire squinted at my JLo dress and Eric's Affleck beard. "Wait. Ben and JLo? Aren't they…?"

"Divorcing. *Allegedly*," I said, waving a hand. "But look at us! We're vibing. He can pull off a faux-beard, I'm his hot Latina muse. It's method acting."

"I see it," Claire said, shrugging like JLo's divorce rumors were just bad Yelp reviews. "And screw the tabloids. Their drama isn't our theme song. We're *Halloween*, baby. Temporary and zero stakes." She might've launched into a TED Talk on celebrity culture, but Marc reappeared, thrusting Ethan at her like a hot potato.

"The guys want to talk UFC stats and manly things," Marc said, gesturing vaguely toward Jason and Eric, who were now comparing bicep tattoos. "Can you take Ethan? The carrier's in the car. I'll help strap him on. It's like a backpack, right?"

Claire gave him a death glare. "Jason's over there juggling Rubi and a latte like dad of the year, but sure, *you* need a break." She hoisted Ethan onto her hip, muttering, "Next year, I'm dressing him as a fanny pack."

As she lugged Ethan toward Cali—now parked like a beached whale in the corner—Claire's face softened. "Hey, due date up-and-comer. Comparing stretch marks or plotting world domination?"

Cali grinned. "Mostly wondering if I can charge people to rub my belly for luck. Baby's a cash cow, Claire."

By midnight, the crowd had thinned to just the die-hards: Felicia stress-eating leftover "finger" tarts, Shane napping in the Pooh crop top, and Eric, who'd traded his Affleck beard for a smolder that could melt polar ice caps.

"So," he said, sidling up to me, "apparently we're doomed because Ben and JLo are 'over'?" His arms slid around my waist, scratchy beard tickling my neck. "Think the universe is trying to tell us something?"

"Only that people who believe in celebrity gossip probably also buy horoscopes and healing crystals," I said, leaning into him. "We're fine. Cute Latina, hot himbo—it's a classic rom-com trope."

"Himbo?" He gasped. "I'll have you know I read *War and Peace* last week."

"The graphic novel edition doesn't count," I teased.

He laughed, nuzzling my temple. "Next year, we're going as Eva Mendes and Ryan Gosling. No drama, just good times."

"Deal," I said, ignoring the tiny voice in my head that whispered, "Why didn't I think of that *this* year."

CHAPTER

SEVENTEEN

THE DESERT NIGHT WAS so cold, even the cacti were shivering. There we were, huddled under outdoor heaters that were clearly designed by someone who'd never left Florida, clutching frozen margaritas like they were hand warmers. Cali's backyard had become our Arctic survival camp—complete with cozy blankets, gossip, and a debate about brown sugar that was heating up faster than Lexi's dating history.

"Black molasses and white sugar make brown sugar!" I announced, tired of the back and forth.

Lexi gasped, nearly spilling her drink. "Lies! Brown sugar is *obviously* crushed jaggery. It's, like, a spiritual sweetener. I had it in Dubai with this guy who owned a jaggery empire— or was it a yacht? Anyway, he flew me first class, and the flight attendant served it with gold spoons." She paused, wistful. "We broke up because he said my aura clashed with his sugarcane farm."

(Translation: Her demands were higher than his budget—his romantic budget, that is.)

Felicia snorted. "Eva's right. Brown sugar is just white sugar's tanned cousin. I taught her that when she tried to bake cookies that could've doubled as hockey pucks."

"Hey, those cookies had character," I protested. "And they were gluten-free!"

"So is cement," Felicia shot back.

Lexi slumped, her designer puffer jacket crinkling like a defeated potato chip bag. "My whole life is a lie. Next you'll tell me truffle oil isn't made by actual truffle-hunting pigs!"

The conversation devolved into a sugar-fueled chaos, as all great girls' nights do. Lexi ranted about jaggery's "earthy vibes," Felicia teased me about my brief stint as a "baker," and I marveled at how we'd gone from discussing sweeteners to airing generational grievances.

"At least your mom's a stripper," Felicia muttered, apropos of nothing. "Mine texts me Harvard Law Review articles and signs them 'Love, Mom.'"

Lexi perked up. "Yours sends articles? Mine just sends Venmo requests."

It was a rare moment of truce. Lexi's mom, a retired pole-dancing queen, wanted her to "marry rich and retire richer," while Felicia's mom, a corporate lawyer who'd probably negotiated her own C-section, viewed the café as a "quaint phase." And me? My mom still thought "independent woman" was a real job.

As the margaritas flowed, so did the camaraderie. We toasted to dysfunctional families, questionable life choices, and the fact that—despite Lexi's insistence—brown sugar was, indeed, *not* magic.

"To generational curses taking a spa day," I said, raising my glass.

"And to Eva not burning down the café," Felicia added.

Claire leaned forward, eyes narrowed like a detective interrogating a suspect. "Rumor has it you're giving up your stake in the café. Please tell me that's just Lexi spreading lies again."

I sipped my margarita, happy with my choice. "Dramatic much? I'm not 'giving up' anything. I'm repositioning my portfolio."

"Repositioning your—" Claire sputtered, gesturing wildly at Felicia and Lexi, who were snickering into their drinks like Shakespearean henchmen. "You're letting Felicia buy you out? After everything?!"

"Buy me *in*," I corrected. "I'm an investor now. Less paperwork, more perks. I still get a cut of the pumpkin spice profits *and* veto power on Felicia's 'experimental' lattes."

Claire blinked. "But why?"

"Because running a café is like dating a high-maintenance cactus. It's prickly, it's needy, and it will drain your bank account." I shrugged. "I'm better at the fun stuff. Like convincing UFC fighters to fund my side quests."

Felicia raised her glass. "She's basically our retired rockstar. Shows up for the encore, avoids the soundcheck."

Claire wasn't buying it. "And the salaries? How are you covering—"

"Savings, side hustles, and a stellar ability to ignore my credit card statements," I said breezily. "Besides, after 'UFC Scare Night'? Honey, I could sell sand to a camel. Those meet-and-greets funded my entire winter coat budget."

"We live in Vegas," Claire chimed in.

I shrugged. "Exactly."

Across the patio, Cali let out a snore so loud it startled a coyote. Her swollen feet were propped on a stack of pillows, her belly rising and falling like an over proofed sourdough loaf. Baby Boy was now four days late, and Cali had resorted to every wives' tale in existence: 1) Bouncing on a yoga ball like a deranged kangaroo. 2) Eating spicy wings while muttering, "Evict yourself, tiny squatter." 3) "Romantic walks" that devolved into Jason pushing her in a wheelbarrow.

"She swore she wasn't tired," Lexi whispered, snapping a photo of Cali mid-snort. "This is going in the baby shower slideshow."

"Let her sleep," I said, tucking a blanket over Cali's toes. "She's been training for a marathon nobody signed her up for."

Claire had morphed into a pregnancy watchdog, poking Cali's blanket burrito every 20 minutes like it was a suspicious parcel. "Is she breathing? Should we check her pulse? What if she goes into labor mid-snore?"

"Claire, *relax*," I said, rearranging Cali's mountain of blankets. "Pregnant women aren't made of porcelain. They're more like… extremely cozy grenades. She's fine. Let her hibernate. Soon she'll be up every hour singing lullabies to a tiny dictator."

"But it's freezing—"

"She's got a heater, three quilts, and a belly the size of a minivan. She's living her best rotisserie chicken life."

Claire finally backed off, and I plopped back into my chair, nursing my margarita like a therapist. "Why is everyone auditing my life choices but giving Lexi a free pass on the Scott saga? She's the one dating a human golden raisin!"

Felicia smirked. "Because rich old guys are boring, and your Eric stories? *Chef's kiss*. Last week alone, you mentioned biceps, a fireman's carry, and a very detailed shower anecdote."

The group nodded in unison, eyes glittering like they'd just binge-watched a rom-com.

I groaned. "I shared one shower story! And it was about water pressure!"

"Sure, Eva," Lexi purred. "And *Love Island* is about 'friendship.'"

"Fine!" I threw my hands up. "Since we're airing grievances—what's the tea on Scott? Is Charles' still buying you Scott's life savings to compensate for his vintage energy?"

"Age is just a number, Eva!"

"And his number is 'Medicare eligible,'" I muttered, and the girls laughed. "With raisin hands."

"You can mock his life choices," Felicia interjected,

playing referee, "but not his physical attributes. He's still a person."

"Ugh, *fine*." I rolled my eyes. "Lexi, spill."

Lexi groaned, but her smirk betrayed her. She'd been clinging to this gossip like a Kardashian to a selfie stick, waiting for someone to pry it out of her. "So," she relented, leaning in. "Charles finally got through to Scott. And by 'got through,' I mean he bribed Scott's lawyer—who, by the way, makes Saul Goodman look like Mother Teresa—with a case of vintage bourbon and a timeshare in Boca."

Felicia choked on her drink. "Scott's still taking legal advice from a guy who probably defends parking tickets with 'finders keepers'?"

"Desperate times!" Lexi said, waving a manicured hand. "Charles basically told Scott, 'Come home, hire a lawyer who isn't a cartoon villain, and you'll be fine! O.J. walked, baby!'"

"O.J. *Simpson*?" I blurted. "Is Charles suggesting Scott fake a glove allergy too?"

"The point is," Lexi barreled on, "Scott's crimes are white-collar. Nobody cares about rich guys embezzling. It's basically a LinkedIn skill now."

Felicia, ever the voice of reason, frowned. "But what about Tegan? If Scott's MIA, does she get stuck holding his

Gucci bag of debt?"

"Depends," Lexi chirped. "If she claims she thought 'fraud' was just his Wi-Fi password, maybe she gets off for being a bimbo. Her lawyer's begging Scott to man up and face the music, but let's be real—the man married her to frame her. He's not exactly husband-of-the-year material."

Claire, eyes wide as a true-crime podcast addict, sighed. "Who knew gold-digging was this complicated?"

"Literally everyone with a Netflix subscription," Lexi deadpanned.

"True," Claire said, oblivious to the landmine she'd just stomped. "I mean, it's taken you years to lock down Charles. Is he waiting for a Groupon?"

The table froze. Lexi's smile turned lethal, like a Barbie doll holding a shiv. "If it were up to Charles, we'd have been married at the second 'hello.' I'm the one making him earn it. Four prenups, two mistresses, and a—"

"Lexi," I cut in, tossing a lime wedge at her. "No one needs to hear about Charles' 'yacht negotiations' again."

Cali chose that moment to snort-laugh in her sleep, sending her virgin piña colada sloshing perilously close to her belly. The universe's timing, as always, was flawless.

Eric's text lit up my phone, and the photo he sent—those

see-through sweats, clinging in all the right places—nearly made me drop my margarita. I bit my lip, already plotting how to "accidentally" rip them off him later. Sure, I'd probably end up tossed around like a salad, but all in the name of romance. Tomorrow was Saturday: Pilates, Eric's gym selfies (#DeathByDeltoids), and a café meetup where my biggest responsibility would be choosing between oat milk and drama. Perfection.

But Lexi, ever the spotlight hog, was mid-monologue: "I put Charles on pause, took Brody for a test drive, and guess what? Charles came crawling back like a Spanx waistband after Thanksgiving. So don't lecture me about commitment."

Claire, now pale as a ghost who'd just heard its credit score, mumbled, "I was just saying."

"*Juuuust saying,*" Lexi parroted in a voice higher than her heels, margarita sloshing dangerously.

I opened my mouth to defuse things, but Lexi stabbed her phone like it owed her money. "You want answers? Fine. Let's ask Charles."

We all froze. Calling Charles during girls' night was like texting an ex at 2 a.m.—a guaranteed disaster. But Lexi's eyes had gone stormy gray, the same shade as her last boyfriend's hair plugs.

The phone rang twice before Charles answered with a

grunt that could've been a walrus emerging from a nap.

"Baby," Lexi purred, sweetness dripping like expired caramel. "Tell the girls what happens next with us. And don't make me mad, or I'll post those yacht photos."

A muffled groan. Was he stuck in a La-Z-Boy? Running from Interpol? Who knew.

"Don't fret, my sweet," Charles rasped, like a chain-smoking Shakespeare. "Scott's money's practically yours. Just legal red tape. Tiny details."

Lexi's smirk could've powered a small island. "How much money again, darling?"

"A couple, honey. Maybe… three."

"A couple of what?"

"Million. Obviously."

She singsonged. "Thank you. Good night!"

"Good n—" And she hung up.

"Told you. *Cha-ching.*" Lexi crowed, triumphant as a game show host revealing the grand prize. "Straight from the horse's mouth—and by 'horse,' I mean a man who probably still uses AOL, but still. Valid information."

Claire sat frozen, her face the human equivalent of a buffering wheel. Hearing Charles' gravelly "couple million" pledge had clearly short-circuited her brain. To be fair, the man sounded like he'd been dug up from a crypt, but Lexi wasn't wrong—he *did* have a knack for turning dust into diamonds.

Lexi plowed on, detailing her future mansion ("heated floors, obviously"), her prenup-free wedding ("half his fortune, half his Viagra"), and her plans to hire a "hot gardener named Javier." We nodded along like jurors in a courtroom drama, too terrified to interrupt.

Then—silence. Glorious, merciful silence.

Which, of course, is when we heard it: a faint *splish-splash*.

We all swiveled toward the pool, empty except for a lone inflatable flamingo. For a heartbeat, nothing.

Then Felicia shrieked, "Ohmygod, Cali's water broke!"

A margarita glass clattered to the ground. Lexi dropped her phone. Claire began hyperventilating into a napkin. And Cali? Cali blinked awake, glanced at the puddle beneath her chair, and gasped a tiny breath.

Oh, god, I thought. Not again.

AUTHOR'S NOTE

Hi, reader! Thank you for reading my story. I loved getting to know Eva and Eric as a couple, and I hope you loved them too.

If you feel up to it, please sign up to my newsletter by clicking the link below or here. I'm not a spammer, so if you get an email every once in a while when I'm updating on new releases or bonus chapters, then it's something!

Subsribe to Blair's Newsletter

As an indie author, reviews are our lifeline. Please leave a review (if you want to!) on Amazon, Goodreads, or The StoryGraph.

Thank you for supporting me! It means the world.

P.S. Drop a line if you want to be in my ARC Team!
Email at: authorblairmonroy@gmail.com.

Books by Blair Monroy

GIRL FIGHT SERIES

Girl Fight

Spring Blues

Summer Storm

Autumn Falling

About the Author

Blair Monroy writes funny rom-coms with memorable characters who love hard and play hard. When not writing, she's hanging out by the pool with rosé in one hand and a book in the other.

Autumn Falling is the fourth book in the Girl Fight series.

IG: @blairmonroyauthor

TikTok: @authorblairmonroy

Email: authorblairmonroy@gmail.com